Rosenbloom in Love

"The problem with this room," Wendy was saying, "is that there's no place to put my posters. I've sixteen of them, would you believe it? There's no way I can put them all on the walls. What do you think of the ceiling...?"

On the ceiling. She was looking at the ceiling.

"What do you think of that idea?"

"Fantastic." He was on his feet, but he couldn't straighten up completely. Move! Get over there! But then everything went wrong. The room was too small. He was too big. He was moving, but it was as if he'd been shot out of a cannon. He flew across the room—he couldn't stop himself—and fell flat on top of her.

"What the!" She shoved him back. "Get off me, you big ox!"

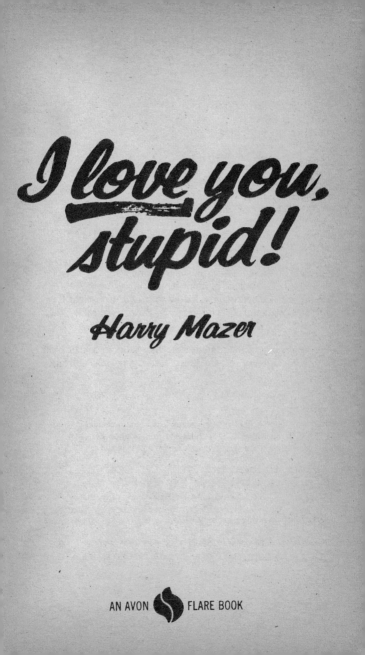

I love you, stupid!

Harry Mazer

AN AVON FLARE BOOK

Cover photograph by Matthew Tepper

AVON BOOKS
A division of
The Hearst Corporation
1790 Broadway
New York, New York 10019

The Harper & Row, Publishers, Inc. edition contains the
following Library of Congress Cataloging in Publication
Data:

Mazer, Harry.
I love you, stupid!
SUMMARY: High school senior Marcus Rosenbloom decides
to cross the wall that divides childhood from adulthood,
but finds it's not the simple matter he thought it would
be.
    I. Title.
PZ7.M47397lal   1981   [Fic]   81—43033
                                   AACR2

First Flare Printing, January, 1983

"Every day of my life I think about getting back into bed.

"Every day of my life I think about what I'm going to do with my life.

"Every day of my life I think about girls."

—From Marcus Rosenbloom's
notebook

I

Entering the school cafeteria, Marcus imagined that girls all over the room were looking up at him. Standing apart this way, on top of the steps, tall, an inch over six feet, made taller by a mass of curly dark hair, he observed— and was observed (he hoped). *"Who's that stunning guy, that senior?" "Look who just came in . . . Isn't he gorgeous?" "Oh, god, it's Marcus Rosenbloom. He's a writer, you know, only seventeen and so brilliant . . . Sexy!"*

He moved aside to let a couple of girls pass, giving them a lingering look. Both were in tight jeans and sweaters, their hair identical—long, curly, and loose. The one nearest him gave him a gorgeous smile.

He followed her with his eyes. She was perfect. God, how he loved the way she moved. He swallowed hard. Why hadn't he smiled back? A dialogue would have started. No words needed . . . her warm interested glance . . . his responsive friendly smile . . . a nod of his head . . . the wink of her butt. In little movements it would begin. Finally. At last. Saved. Redeemed. His life justified. *Sex.*

Seventeen, a high-school senior, nearly a man: he'd been ready for years and he'd never had sex. What was wrong with him? He loved girls. He couldn't stop thinking about them, watching, wanting, lusting. Twelve-year-old boys did it. What was wrong with him?

There was a wall that divided the world, and it wasn't the Chinese Wall, or the Iron Curtain, or even the Wailing Wall in Jerusalem, though sometimes he thought it was most like that wall. The wall he was talking about divided childhood from adulthood. It was first-time sex, and the sex thereafter. It was a wall you didn't even know existed when you were little, but when you found out about it you wanted to know more and more about it. He knew there were more important things in life than sex, but right now he couldn't think what they were.

He looked around the cafeteria, leaning against the railing, smiling slightly as if he saw somebody or had thought of something interesting. He took his notebook from his hip pocket. "Steamy, hot, and noisy." Did that catch the essence of cafeteria bedlam? Maybe "the hot hungry mouths of Sherwood High" was better? He jotted them both down. The Writer at work, too busy for sex.

A girl sitting alone at a nearby table was looking at him. Was it sympathy he saw on her face? He looked around for Alec. His friend loved school lunches. Maybe that had something to do with Alec's success with girls? Marcus never ate school lunch, and he was a failure. Was there something about the breaded fishburgers? Did girls go crazy when they smelled corn dodgers on a guy's breath? Maybe it was something you'd never think of, like the watery green beans. Who knew what turned a girl on? He was probably ruining his chances by not eating this slop, doing himself grievous harm.

His obituary flashed through his mind. DEATH COMES TO A PROMISING YOUNG AUTHOR. He'd be discovered after he died. Some of his brief but brilliant writings would be published. And at his funeral, five hundred grieving girls in white would toss red roses on his coffin.

That girl was still looking at him. He stole a look back. There was something familiar about her, the way her hair stood out around her head like a bright wiry halo. She had a book propped open in front of her. Reading alone, sitting at a table surrounded by noisy barbarians—now that took guts.

Marcus was intrigued. Who was she? Did he know her? He should know her. New girl in school, of course, sitting alone, hiding behind a book: a familiar, even a classic situation. And here he was, the thoughtful, interested, literate senior, looking at her, trying to catch the title of her book. She was reading and spooning lemon-yellow Jello from a dish without looking. Up came the spoon. In a second she was going to have Jello in her nose, but at the last moment the spoon went straight into her mouth. Marcus admired her skill. Bravo!

The girl looked up. "Marcus?"

"Wendy?" he said at the same moment. It couldn't be! Wendy Barrett, the companion of his childhood. It was too much of a coincidence. He'd known Wendy all his life. Their mothers had been best friends. Wendy and he had played together when they were little. There was a photo of the two of them in their underpants, holding hands in a field of buttercups. Wendy and her mother had moved away several years ago, and he hadn't seen her since then. "Wendy?" he said again. She had gained weight, had shoulders and boobs, and looked solid in jeans and a shirt. He saw it all in a glance.

"Marcus?" she said. "Marcus, is that *you*, Marcus Rosenbloom?" She stood up and grabbed him around the neck. It was pure melodrama. Her eyes glistened; a yellow fleck of Jello quivered on her lip. The bell rang and they walked through the cafeteria and into the hall together. She kept looking at him, squeezing his hand and smiling emotionally.

"What are you doing here?" he said.

"I'm here in school, at Sherwood."

"I thought you were in Buffalo."

"I was. I moved back a week ago. I'm living here with my Aunt Ginny and Uncle Doug."

After that first moment of recognition he kept getting a blurred picture of Wendy, a double image, seeing the Wendy he had known superimposed on this new mature Wendy. The voice was unchanged, and the hair and the face too, but she was different. He remembered Wendy, but who was *this* Wendy? The old Wendy was always a little kooky. She dressed oddly and said things that nobody else said. What kind of person was she now? She wore

4

an ankh, a symbol of life, on a silver chain around her neck.

"The last time I saw you there was something dead hanging on a string around your neck," he said.

"I believe it," Wendy said. "I would have recognized you anywhere, Marcus. Did you see me staring at you in the cafeteria? I couldn't be sure, but those blue eyes, Marcus, and those red juicy lips—" She laughed. "Who else could it be?"

Marcus walked Wendy to her class, and they agreed to meet after school.

He was late for Mr. Sweeny's honors course in Advanced Writing. It was a small class, only twelve handpicked students, who met in a conference room, the sort of course they'd be taking in college. They could smoke if they wanted to, or get up and walk around. They were being treated like adults. Phony as hell, but Marcus loved it. He dug around in his pockets for his nail clippers, then settled down next to Bev Kruger and started trimming his nails.

"Do you have to do that?" Bev gave him a pained look. Bev was plump and freckled, with smoky green eyes that turned cat yellow when she looked at him.

"Sorry." That was the usual extent of their conversation. Bev complained and he apologized. She was one of a dozen girls he would have liked to know better . . . know bedder . . . much bed-der . . . Those round arms. She was like a ripe, juicy Florida orange, like whipped cream and chocolate flecks. He could see the freckles through her blouse. Was she freckled all over, and would she unbutton her blouse and show him if he had the nerve to ask? His eyes blurred with wanting as he thought of the two of them together.

"What's going on?" he asked, playing the fool. "What's Sweeny saying? Did I miss anything? What's the assignment? Say, do you have an extra sheet of paper?" He rattled on like a ten-minute quiz. He wanted to know Bev better, but she was always annoyed with him. Even as she gave him a sheet of paper, he felt he'd done something wrong— sat too close, breathed, used up some of her personal air.

Why did he find her so appealing? She was female— what else—and sexy.

He leaned toward Bev. "I just saw Wendy Barrett. I haven't seen her in three years."

"Who's she?"

"A girl I used to know. She's here in Sherwood High." He looked at Bev with engaging utter sincerity. He was talking about a girl he was friends with. I'm safe, he was saying. No matter what you think, I'm really not a madman.

"Wendy Barrett?" Bev said. "I never heard of her."

"We grew up together." Another Mr. Clean remark.

"Mr. Rosenbloom, if you please," Mr. Sweeny said.

Marcus winced and pocketed his nail clippers. "Sorry, Mr. Sweeny."

Sweeny was a spare, nervous man with a reputation for being sharp-tongued. "Ladies and gentlemen, I asked to see a piece of your writing this week. If you will take the time to concentrate, you may remember this is a class in Advanced Writing. I asked to see a sketch, a character study. I have some of your work in hand. However, others! Mr. Rosenbloom?"

"It's coming," Marcus said. "I left it home."

Bev flashed him a yellow-cat look. Marcus blushed. He always blushed when he lied. He hadn't done the assignment. He knew it, Bev knew it, and he was sure Sweeny knew it. Marcus could never tell what Sweeny thought of him. Did he think Marcus was a writer? Did Marcus think Marcus was a writer? He loved to write, to put things into words, he loved the idea of being a writer. Everyone said they were something. His friend Alec was an actor. Pfeff was an activist—he was going to make the world better. Gordy was probably going to be a professor. And Marcus was going to be a writer.

Was it true? Or was it all part of his act: playing the intellectual with the notebook, the heavy reading, and the pipe in his mouth? In tenth grade Mrs. Granenstein had read some of his poems to the class in her sexy, sandy voice. Did that make him a writer? Did a few things published in the school literary rag make him one? He was afraid he was a blowhard, self-inflating, a hot-air balloon. All talk and no action, like his sex life, all make-believe. He was still in kiddie land dreaming about the great things he was going to do. And what had he done? Nothing.

Mr. Sweeny pinned him down. "I know you have a big reputation as a writer to uphold. I'll expect something impressive."

Bev was looking at Marcus. He felt the whole class looking at him. "It will knock your eyes out, sir."

7

2

A girl was waiting for him. Marcus saw Wendy standing at the far end of the corridor. Too bad it wasn't Bev Kruger. He no longer recognized Wendy. So they'd known each other years ago. What did that mean now? They'd been kids then. What did they have in common now? They'd meet. She'd say, *Marcus.* He'd say, *Wendy.* Great conversation. *"How's your mother?"* *"Fine, how's yours?"* And then what?

"Marcus," she said, as he approached.

"Wendy." Great. Next she'd say, *How's your mother?*

"How's your mother?"

"Fine, how's yours." Rolling his eyes, he pushed open

8

the door. This was going to be pure adolescent torment.

Outside, the wind struck them in the face. Marcus was jacketless. *Rugged individualism.* The wind found the holes in his jeans. *Modest poverty.* Wendy wore a boy's red plaid jacket, Bean boots, jeans. Was that her new costume, the new kookiness? Not very kooky. The old Wendy was a lot more interesting.

"You look like you're ready to go backpacking," he said.

"I'd love to. How about you?"

Enthusiastic type. "Me? I can take it or leave it."

"If you haven't done it, don't knock it. Nobody should talk till they've tried it."

Jumps to conclusions. "When I was fourteen," he said slowly, with satisfaction, "I spent a whole summer back-packing—living outdoors, canoeing through Algonquin Provincial Park in Ontario, Canada."

"Your mother let you?"

"Why shouldn't she?"

"You were only fourteen."

"She couldn't stand having me around. I used to dribble a basketball in the apartment and set off thermal explosions on the windowsill. I was a royal pain in the ass. My whole character has been retooled since then."

They crossed over toward Meadowbrook. There were still patches of snow on the ground, dirty mounds of it pushed to the edges of the parking lot. Marcus set a fast pace. *Olympic style.* He wasn't going to slow down for her; let her run and keep up. She did keep up! *Show-off.*

"You're taller," she said.

"You too." They were back to kindergarten talk.

"And thinner. Much thinner."

So she'd noticed. *An observant type*. The last of the fat had disappeared that summer in Algonquin. But once fat you never forget. "I lost five or six hundred pounds canoeing."

"Come on, Marcus, you were never that fat."

She says nice things too. "Your memory fails you."

"No, my memory is fine. I remember you very well. We always had fun. You were the only sane person I knew."

Sane? Nice? Was that what he was. "I should have been crazier."

"Why would you want to be crazy?" Wendy said.

Takes everything too seriously. "Did you ever know a writer who wasn't a little peculiar?"

"I don't know any writers."

"Now you do. *I am a writer.*"

"You?"

Shock and surprise. "What did you think I'd be?"

"A pharmacist. No, I'm joking. You look more the doctor type. I thought a writer needed a lot of imagination."

"Thanks a lot." *Tactless twit.*

"I shouldn't have said that, should I?"

"Say whatever you please." He dropped back so he was behind her and checked her out. *All right.* She was still a stupid snit.

She took his arm. "Don't tell me to say anything I want to. That's how I get into trouble. I don't know when to stop talking sometimes. Have you noticed?"

"No. Oh, no." *Not you, Miss Leaky Faucet.*

"I do talk a lot. Whatever I think of I say. That's indiscreet. Did I make you mad?"

"Mad? No, I never lose my cool."

"Because I said that about imagination? But really, I never thought you'd be a writer."

Drip, drip, drip.

"If after all these years we had a fight the first time we met, that would be depressing. Sherwood's been depressing enough."

"This high school," he said, "can be pretty hard to take if you're not used to it. It's a factory."

"Oh, I suppose so. Coming to a new school in my senior year—it's tough making friends."

What was he letting himself in for? Was that what she was fishing for? Was he going to be her friend, her guide through Sherwood Forest? Stout-hearted Marcus. Did he need it? He didn't. He had enough friends.

"If I sound like I'm whining," Wendy said, "I'm not. I know everything will work out."

Well put, Wendy, very well put. Keep a stiff upper lip and good things will come to you. But not good Marcus Rosenbloom.

A jogger in a gray sweat suit passed them in the road. "See that man?" Wendy said. "He reminds me of Steve, the man my mother is living with."

"Your stepfather."

"Steve's not my stepfather. Please, not that. He's my mother's lover. We didn't get along from Day One. There's nothing I do he likes, and I don't like him either. He's a fanatic. You should see him, Marcus, out jogging every day, no matter what. Can you stand people who are so disciplined? He was in the army. Rise at precisely six A.M., in the bathroom for precisely twenty minutes, doing precisely what he's supposed to."

Yes, Marcus could imagine himself that way. Up at six, in the bathroom for precisely twenty minutes, then calisthenics for ten minutes, writing for thirty minutes, more exercise (keep the brain flooded with blood), more writing, more exercise. . . . He'd love to follow a schedule like that, but he knew he could never stick to it for more than thirty seconds.

Wendy, once she started talking about Steve, grew more and more intense. "One day I said to Steve, 'Why don't you get Sweet Life'—that's what he calls her—'why don't you get Sweet Life out there jogging with you?' 'Why don't you get out there yourself,' he said. That's the way we are—cat and dog. I only said it because I thought my mother could use some exercise. She's got the same problem I have: too much weight below the waist. And she teaches all day and doesn't exercise. I don't know if you've noticed, Marcus, but I'm like two different people. I'm fine on top, but from the waist down I have problems. Am I saying too much?"

"No, no," he said. *Thoughtful, Dr. Marcus. Keep on babbling, Miss Brooks.*

"Maybe Steve was trying to tell me something, but I reacted. He says every time I open my mouth there's trouble, and he's probably right. I've always been that way. With my mother too. We fight over everything. You remember that, Marcus. We'd fight, but then we'd make up and cry on each other's shoulder. But with Steve it was like World War III."

"Is that why you left?"

"It really got to be awful, Marcus. Mom didn't want me to go, but it was so depressing, I had to leave." Wendy stopped. "This probably bores you. Well—" She gestured to a high privet hedge. "Time to stop. This is where I live."

He remembered the narrow yellow house with the driveway on one side and the lawn on the other. He'd been here once or twice with his mother, but the swings, a sandbox, and jungle gym were unfamiliar, and so was the sign out front: Happy Days Playschool.

"It's small," Wendy said. "Practically the whole house is for the playschool, except for the kitchen and their bedroom. The room I'm in used to be the pantry. It's tiny, but nice."

He stood there waiting to get away. Maybe they'd see each other again. *See you in school . . . see you around . . . see you next week. . .*

"Well," they said simultaneously. She grabbed his hand and linked pinkies.

"What goes up a chimney?"

They were back to nursery school now.

"What goes up a chimney?" she repeated.

"I don't know," he said.

"You're slow. Smoke. And what comes down a chimney?"

"Soot."

"And perverse. You ruined it. The answer is Santa Claus. Do you want to say hello to my aunt? She'll like to see you. She knows your mother."

"Not really," he muttered to himself. "I can only stay a minute," he said aloud.

Aunt Ginny was on the lawn side of the house, surrounded by children bundled up in jackets, hats, and mittens. He could see the resemblance between Wendy and her Aunt Ginny. No makeup, the same round face, the same blond wiry hair. Aunt Ginny's was pulled back with a shoelace. "Marcus Rosenbloom?" she said. "I suppose I should remember you." She reached for a cigarette in her jacket pocket. "Sorry."

"No problem," Marcus said. He didn't remember her, either.

"I'm going to show Marcus my room, Ginny. Okay?"

"Okay with me. You kids! Stop shoving. Nate, you come over here by me."

Wendy's room. That was cool of her, asking him in to meet her aunt, then taking him to her room. What next? Was he going to discover something about this new Wendy he hadn't even let himself guess before? Didn't she know about his perverted appetites? She'd always been something of a witch, a spider luring him into her web, and he, the pure-minded, helpless, hairy, little six-foot monster.

Wendy's room had an outside door at the back of the house. Up three steps and you were in. "My own private entrance," she said. There was a sign in the window that said Hello. Now this was starting to get interesting. When was the last time a girl had invited him into her room? The answer, after a moment's quick calculation, was never.

The room was just big enough for a bed and a small table and chair. "I love it," Wendy said. "Isn't it cozy?" She fell back on the bed. "You're my first guest. I hope you feel suitably honored."

"Oh, yes, yes. Honored . . . honored guest." He sat down on the chair and grimaced. He could hardly sit straight because Good King George had jumped up the moment she fell on the bed. He wasn't thinking too clearly either. She was lying with her hands behind her head, her jeans tight across her thighs.

He couldn't believe where he was, the opportunity that was suddenly being offered him. He'd heard about girls like this, friendly and easy to talk to when you met them outside, but once they got you in their room . . . *Opportunity strikes but once.* There was less than two feet between them, but it could have been two hundred miles. Step across, he told himself. But how? If how had been in the sex manual, he'd missed it.

"It's small, but I love the privacy," she said aloud.

Underneath he heard her challenge. *Your move, old chap.* Move, he told himself. What he had to do was stand up . . .

"The problem with this room," Wendy was saying, "is that there's no place to put my posters. I've got sixteen of them, would you believe it? There's no way I can put them all on the walls. What do you think of the ceiling? I have one from Switzerland that would fit perfectly."

On the ceiling. She was looking at the ceiling.

"What do you think of that idea?"

"Fantastic." He was on his feet, but he couldn't straighten up completely. Move! Get over there! But then everything went wrong. The room was too small. He was too big. He was moving, but it was as if he'd been shot out of a cannon. He flew across the room—he couldn't stop himself—and fell flat on top of her.

"What the!" She shoved him back. "Get off me, you big ox."

He scrambled back. He couldn't get away fast enough.

She sat up. He retreated to the door, stammering and apologizing. There was an expression on her face he couldn't meet. "What was that all about?" she demanded.

"You said—"

"What did I say? I didn't say anything."

"Wait a minute," he said. "Just let me explain."

"Okay, you explain it."

He took a breath. His voice shook. Did she notice? "I— I thought—"

"Thought what?"

"You know, when you said come see my room." It sounded so stupid now.

"So is that the way it was? Just because I said come see my room." His face burned. "You thought wrong."

"I know it now." He leaned against the door. He wished he could fall through it and disappear.

"I never thought I'd get into a wrestling match with you, Marcus. I never thought it, not for a second. I thought we were old friends."

"We are, we are." What did she expect? He wasn't thirteen years old anymore, and neither was she.

"I don't think this is the way you act with a friend."

"You do with girl friends." He tried a smile. She didn't respond.

"I'm not your girlfriend."

"Right, right, it was stupid, I know. I'm sorry. Wrong signals." How long was this bloodletting going to go on?

"I don't want to be stupid about this either," she said, "but I didn't think—I really thought we were friends."

"We are, we are."

"Are we?"

"Yes, we're friends."

"Okay," she said, "let's forget it then."

No smile. Did she believe him? He didn't dare offer his hand. Go, he told himself. This is not your finest hour. Still he lingered. He didn't want her to think that all he had on the brain was sex. There was more to him than that. It was a matter of pride. "I'm not this way all the time."

"I hope not."

"Are we friends again?"

"Sure," she said, and raised two fingers in the peace sign.

He wiped his forehead in relief. *Good sport. Knows how to take a joke. Great pair of boobs too.*

Suddenly Wendy pointed. "Look." A little face had appeared at the window, then another, then a third. "They're spying on us."

"The Martians have landed." Marcus leaped up flapping his arms. The faces disappeared from the window.

"Mean!" Wendy said.

"That's me," Marcus agreed. "Big, baaad, mean Marcus."

3

On the way home Marcus stopped at Cherry Street to see Alec. He wanted to talk to him about what had happened with Wendy. What *had* happened? He'd so utterly misread all the cues. He'd gotten near a girl and done things he didn't even know he was going to do. Could he trust himself near a girl anymore? He wanted Alec, who was Mr. Smooth and Languid around girls, to reassure him that what he'd done wasn't that bad. But from the minute Alec came to the door it was jokes and they never got to anything. It was always jokes when he and Alec got together.

"Christ, look at you," Marcus said. Alec wore white

pants, a tight electric blue nylon shirt, and boots with two-inch heels.

"Hello, my boy." Alec pulled on his Eisenhower jacket. "I'm on my way to the tryouts for *Our Town*. Wait till you see who's picking me up—pure Hollywood stock." Alec looked like Hollywood himself. With his dark skin, high cheekbones, and soft eyes, he looked like a romantic lead in an old movie. Glamour the Actor.

"I've come to confess," Marcus said. "I just went over the edge."

"Confess, my boy." Alec clamped a hand on Marcus's shoulder and put the squeeze on till Marcus winced.

"It's about a girl."

"I know, my son. Who is she?"

"My lips are sealed." But then Marcus said, "I was in her room."

"Excellent beginning!"

"Thank you, Professor Smut." Jokes. "I was on top of her."

"Good, good!"

"Then she screamed."

"Bad, bad."

"I got all the signals wrong." It hurt Marcus to say it, but he kept on. "What is it about me that terrifies girls, Dr. Dirty?"

"It's that hairy head of yours."

"It's bad, Alec, very bad."

"No, no, my boy, don't take it so much to heart." Alec patted him on the arm and looked down the street for his ride.

The unfairness of it struck Marcus. Here was Alec looking for his California beauty, and here he was spilling out another pathetic failure.

"You're coming to the audition with me," Alec said. "I want you to clap like a maniac."

"I might come," Marcus said, "and I might not."

Alec pulled a silver cigarette case from his jacket pocket. "Damn it to hell, Rosenbloom. You're not coming, Gordy's not coming, and Pfeff's not sure. Some friends I've got."

"Please, Canale, I can't stand it when you weep. I didn't say I wouldn't come. I said I might not come. Note the difference."

"You're coming then. Good, very good, my boy. I need all the help I can get."

"That's what I've been telling you all your life."

The Hollywood beauty drove up in a sporty white Datsun. "Product of California" was written all over her. Alec greeted her. "Hi, Terri. Nervous about tonight? I always am. This is my friend Marcus. Terri's from Los Angeles, California."

"Anaheim," Terri said, and gave Marcus a very straight, interested, unemotional look. Nothing nervous about her.

Marcus stuck out his hand. "Pleased to meet you." The rising young executive in torn Levis. "I'm splitting," he said to Alec.

"Wait a minute, what's your rush? You want to give this poor sap a ride home?"

"Why not?" Terri said, and gave Marcus another interested look.

Marcus got in back. "Which way?" Terri said.

"He knows the way." Alec caressed Terri's neck, and Marcus, like a voyeur, couldn't tear his eyes away. Why was it so easy for Alec and so hard for him? He felt such a tug of envy, despair, and anger that he reached over and mashed Alec's shoulder, really put the squeeze on him.

"You moron, cut that out!"

"What's the matter, can't take it?"

"Boys," Terri said. "I thought you were friends."

Alec rubbed his shoulder. "You have to forgive my friend, Terri. Near a pretty girl he goes over the edge."

Over the edge . . . The whole thing at Wendy's washed over Marcus, humiliated him all over again. He sank back and looked out the window. Why had he said anything to Alec?

At his house he got out quickly. "Thanks," he said in his deepest, manliest tones. As he went upstairs, he began to feel really crappy. First there was that stupid remark in Sweeny's class about knocking his eyes out, then the gorilla act with Wendy, and now coming on like the Flying Hulk in front of this stunning girl. What idiot thing was he going to do next?

"Lamb chop," his grandmother May greeted him when he walked into the apartment. "Come here and kiss me, darling. I brought you a present."

Marcus kissed his grandmother, then greeted his mother, who was leaning against a table pinning her hair up. She'd changed from her downtown workclothes into a pair of comfortable pants and one of Marcus's old white T-shirts.

"Aren't you going to ask me what your present is?" his grandmother said.

"Okay, Grandma, what's my present?" Only she could

baby him in that way and get away with it.

"Lamb chops for my lamb chop."

"Oh, well, thanks." He was getting a little old to be thrilled by food. "How are you, Grandma? How are you feeling?" He worried about her. She was old and she acted like a teenager. She had a boyfriend; in fact she'd just gotten a new one. She was dressed like an airline hostess, in a blue pants suit, with a blue silk scarf around her neck.

"Marcus," his mother said, "what do you want with your lamb chops?"

He felt a spurt of anger. "Are they just for me? Am I the only one eating lamb chops? If I am, forget it."

"I'm sorry, Markey," his grandmother said. "I only bought two chops, they're so expensive. You used to love them when you were little."

"We can share them."

"Of course," his mother said soothingly. "There's nothing to get worked up about." Calming the beast. "I thought we'd have a salad and thaw some peas and carrots."

Food again! Couldn't they stop talking about food? "Good! Fine! I'll eat whatever's on the table. Don't we have anything else to talk about? Is that what we've sunk to? How about a little spritely conversation? 'How was your day, Sally?' 'Fine, thank you, Marcus, how was yours?' 'Couldn't be better, thank you, one thrill after another!'" He stopped. He was going over the edge again. His mother's face . . . Sally turned and without a word walked out, then called from the kitchen. "Ma, you're going to eat with us."

"Am I invited?"

Sally reappeared and looked hard at Marcus. "Did I

say that wrong too? What is it in this family? Doesn't anyone know how to say yes or no anymore? *Yes, you are invited, Ma.*" She sat down and reached for a book. "No rush, I'll wait till you two are ready."

Go to your room, he told himself. Shut the door quietly and do that work for Sweeny. Go before you say or do something you will regret. The whole weekend will be down the drain if you don't start now. But his mother's anger was like a chain that held him in place.

"Where were you?" she said. "I thought it was your turn to get things ready for supper?"

"I stopped at Alec's." He could have said something about Wendy—Sally and Wendy's mother were old friends—but it seemed too complicated. "I have to do some work for Sweeny's class," he said. "I better get started. I'm going out later."

"Where, if I'm not being too inquisitive?"

"Maybe you are?" May said. "He could be meeting a girl. I'd go with him in a minute if I was a girl again."

"Not my son, Ma. He's waiting for the perfect girl. Marcus is a perfectionist. With him everything is black and white."

"You don't know me." He was on the edge of really being disagreeable and saying something he'd be sorry for later. And then he did—said something he was sorry for. "As a matter of fact," he said to his mother, "I *am* going with a girl."

They both looked at him. "Really," his grandmother said.

"What's her name?" Sally said, and smiled. That did it. She thought he was faking it.

"As a matter of fact, it's Wendy."

23

"Who?" his mother said.

"Wendy," he said again. "Wendy Barrett."

"Wendy *Barrett!*"

Now he'd stuck his foot in it. He'd have to call Wendy and ask her to go to the audition with him, and what if she didn't want to—as she probably didn't.

"You're not talking about Grace's Wendy?" Marcus nodded. "Wendy's here? Is Grace here too? Where'd you see her?"

"Wendy's here alone, living with her aunt and uncle over on Victoria Place. She couldn't stand her mother's boyfriend so she left."

"Wait a minute." Sally put a hand on Marcus's arm. "When did all this happen?"

Marcus shrugged. "I don't know. I just met Wendy today." He turned to his grandmother. "Tell me about this new boyfriend."

May lit a cigarette. "A very nice man. He lives in my building. We've been playing Scrabble every Tuesday night."

"Does your new boyfriend like you smoking, Grandma?"

"Nobody asked him. He likes me the way I am. Don't look so surprised, darling. At this age you get wrinkles, but you also get weak eyes so you don't see the wrinkles. To my friend Gary, I'm as gorgeous as Miss America."

"He's handing you a line, Grandma."

"You mean he wants something from me? I should be so lucky. Don't worry, Markey darling." She ruffled his hair. "You're still numero uno with May Rosenbloom."

May stretched out on the couch with her cigarette raised, watching the smoke curl up. "I always loved when the children were little, and I was lying down and they talked and played. Then I knew everything was all right, and I could sleep. So don't you two be afraid to talk and make up." She closed her eyes.

It was awkward for a moment, then Sally said, "I had a letter from Bill today."

Marcus looked at his grandmother. Her eyes were closed. "Where is he? Still in Rio?"

"Right. Buenos Aires next week," Sally said.

Wendy would call Bill Brenner his mother's lover. But to Marcus, who had lived with him and seen him around the house all his life, he was just Bill, his mother's friend— his friend too. When Bill played the trumpet—he was a professional musician—the veins on the side of his bald head stood out like little blue worms, and he wiped his mouth a lot with a handkerchief. He was always going away on tours and returning with presents. The first thing he did when he returned was take off his shoes and socks and lie on the floor and say how good it was to be back home.

"Just think how much better your life would have been if you'd stuck with George," Marcus said.

"George?" For a moment his mother didn't get it. "You mean *George Renfrew*? Your father? Where'd that idea come from?"

"You have to admit your life would have been different."

"It would have been stupid. I wouldn't have stayed with that unfeeling character, not in a million years. The only good thing he ever did was give me you."

"Maybe I ought to go see him again." He was baiting his mother. "I'll take a tape recorder along this time, find out what kind of man he really is."

Marcus had been brought up by his mother. He hadn't

known anything about his father till he was thirteen. Then he had gone looking for him—against his mother's advice—and found him. George Renfrew had another family, another son too, and he was only pained and inconvenienced by the appearance of his first son. Marcus had told himself he'd never think about the man again, but he did sometimes, when he was feeling low.

"There isn't that much of George Renfrew in you." Sally held up her little finger. "Not a fingernail's worth. You've got feeling. He never had a drop of it." She put out her hand. "Here, pull me up. I'm sorry I flipped before." She kissed him. "I'm still an adolescent, right?"

"Worse than I ever was." He embraced his mother.

"Am I going to get to see Wendy sometime?" she asked.

Oh, god, he'd almost forgotten. He had to call Wendy. How was he going to get around that? "I guess so."

"Tell her I want to see her. Tell her to come over this weekend."

"Tell her yourself, Sally. I'm not her answering service." She twisted his ear. "No wonder I feel like wringing your neck sometimes."

"Who?" he said. "Lovable me?"

4

"Hello, Wendy. Guess who?"

"Who?"

"Your friendly neighborhood pervert. No, it's that clean-cut lad."

"Marcus?"

"The one and only. You busy tonight? How'd you like to go to an audition with me?" He'd been sailing along on his own wind up to now, but now the wind died down. The last time he'd asked a girl to go out she'd said, Try again next year.

"A friend of mine is trying out for a part with the Down City Players. It'll be interesting."

"Well," Wendy said, "I was going to wash my hair."

"You can wash your hair another time."

"I don't know. I might have to go shopping with my aunt."

"Look," he said, "is it what happened today? Is that why you don't want to go with me? You still sore about that?"

"No, I'm not. I've forgotten about that."

"Good, then I'll pick you up in fifteen minutes."

"Well, okay, make it a half hour."

Marcus wore jeans, a blue turtleneck, and the same boots he wore everywhere. No affectation. He'd considered wearing a plain gold chain, but decided against it.

"Whose car?" Wendy said as she got in. She was all in green: green cords, a light green embroidered shirt, and a green Army fatigue cap. She was smiling, but he felt a little sweaty with her, unsure, and he started talking too much.

"It's my mother's car. I only got it after I told her who I was picking up. Otherwise, I could have hoofed it."

"Your mother doesn't like to lend you her car?"

"This is the way she thinks I drive." He messed up his hair and stuck his tongue out the side of his mouth. He was sorry the minute he did it. He was acting like a juvenile. Off on the wrong foot again.

"So who's this friend?" she said.

"Alec Canale, a terrific actor. Wait'll you see. If he weren't a damn good friend, I'd never show up for this audition. *Our Town.* I've already seen the bloody play four times. I saw it on TV, then when the junior class put it on, and over at the college once."

"That's only three times," Wendy said.

"Picky, picky." Was this the way it was going to be from now on, a dueling match? Wendy had given him that big smile when she got into the car, but now he wasn't so sure. Was she one of those people who never forgot or forgave?

At Down City they found a seat in back in the old synogogue that had been turned into a theater. Pfeff was already there. Marcus whispered introductions. Wendy leaned forward with that big Barrett smile. Pfeff was wearing a No Nukes T-shirt, and she said she was against it too. Pfeff, who wore glasses and had a nose like a mole, gave her a pained smile. He didn't have a good word to say for any girl. He sank back in his seat next to Marcus and muttered, "Marc-ass, you have hit rock bottom. Where'd you dig that up?"

Marcus gave him an elbow. "Don't talk, you blind bat. It's a friend."

"You could use some enemies."

The director, who was sitting in front, called for quiet, then started calling out the actors. Marcus leaned forward. The empty, poorly lit stage filled him with anticipation. Most of the people trying out were not half bad, but Pfeff was turning thumbs down on everyone. "Hand me a tomato, Marcus." "Throw that one to the lions."

Several girls tried out for Emily's part. Terri was one of the last. When she came out on the stage, Pfeff started hopping around. "Oh, oh, look at those monuments. Capital, capital! She gets the part."

Terri, playing Emily, looked around hesitantly, her hands clasped. "I just can't sleep yet, Papa. The moonlight's so won-der-ful."

Marcus thought she was good, but because Pfeff was there he said, "A little overdone maybe."

"What are you talking about?" Pfeff said. "I told you she gets the part. With an ass like that, who cares if she can act?"

Marcus glanced at Wendy, who was sitting with her lips pressed together. "Wait'll you see Alec," he said to her. Had he made a mistake bringing her? She wasn't going to like anything. But when Alec appeared on stage he couldn't help bragging. "That's Alec. Now you're going to see something special."

Alec had parted his hair in the middle and hooked a pair of red suspenders to his white pants. "Emily, I'm glad you spoke to me about that—that fault in my character." His voice, theatrical, rich, and resonant, sent a shiver down Marcus's spine. "Do you like that?" he said to Wendy. "I told you he was good. You glad you came now?"

"Shh." She folded her legs under her and leaned forward.

"I always made sure where you were sitting on the bleachers," Alec-playing-George said, "and who you were with, and for three days now I've been trying to walk home with you."

After Alec's performance, they all three applauded loudly. People up front looked around. "I'm splitting," Pfeff said. "Our buddy's too good for this decrepit capitalist dream stuff." He nodded to Wendy. "See you."

"I don't like your friend," Wendy said after Pfeff left. "I don't like his attitude toward women."

"Yeah, well." Marcus's loyalties were divided. "He can be rough. Underneath he's really shy."

As they waited for Alec out front on the broad concrete steps, Marcus began to feel uneasy remembering how he'd told Alec about the girl he'd fallen on top of and here he was a few hours later with Wendy. Alec was going to put it together, and maybe say something, and then Wendy would really be convinced that Marcus was an all-American creep. But if Alec caught it, he didn't say anything. He looked at Wendy, looked at Marcus, and then it was all Wendy. "So you're coming to old Sherwood High?"

"Just this year." Wendy twirled her cap. "Then I'm going to the Forestry School."

"Really? Going to be a lumberjack? I'm joking," he said quickly, and pressed her arm. "You don't look like a lumberjack." He really turned on the charm: a lot of eye and hand contact, interested, asking questions. Marcus felt around for his pipe. Alec could touch a girl without making a fool of himself.

"There's more to forestry than cutting trees," Wendy said.

"I know it. It was a callow remark. What aspect of forestry you interested in?"

"Basically, creating green environments in cities."

"Super, that's where we need it. I'm into that. The environment's a mess. Look at this place." He kicked a white plastic cup aside. "We could use a Green Tree demonstration project right here." He snapped his silver cigarette case open and offered Wendy a cigarette.

"I don't smoke," she said almost regretfully. And then "Oh, why not?" She took a cigarette, but just held it. Her eyes lingered on Alec. "I'm sure you're going to get the part. You're so relaxed on stage, so natural."

"Well . . ." Alec blew the smoke away from Wendy. "I hate tryouts. I feel like I'm on the block. Are you interested in theater?"

"I am now." She was glowing.

Just then Terri and another girl came flying down the stairs. "We got it," Terri screamed. "We got the parts!" She kissed Alec on the mouth. "You doll! We did it! I'm Emily and you're George."

Now the other girl kissed Alec. Marcus recognized her as one of the Emilys. "I'm sorry you missed, Pam," Terri kept saying.

"I don't care," Pam said, "as long as I have a part. I don't even care if I get to be the dead girl in the cemetery."

The two girls pulled Alec back up the stairs. "Vanderhoff wants to talk to you."

"Congratulations," Wendy called.

Alec turned back. "Wendy, sorry I have to rush off. I'll see you in school. Let's stay in touch. I like talking to you."

As they walked to the car Marcus said, a little gloomily, "You just made a friend." Terri hadn't even looked at him.

Wendy put her arm through Marcus's. "Two friends. Met an old friend, and made a new one."

"All's forgiven?"

"Oh, that. Of course. I'm glad you called me. It's been a super evening." A flicker of a smile crossed her face. She rolled the cigarette between her fingers. "Alec's got a girlfriend, I suppose?"

"Are you serious, Barrett? You saw those two girls. Alec can't keep the girls off."

"I'm not surprised." She dropped the unlit cigarette into her pocket. "He's such a powerhouse." There was a far-away look on her face.

Marcus busied himself with his pipe. Jesus, he thought, Alec has made another conquest.

5

"I want you to drive Wendy home after supper," Sally said.

"Do I get the car?"

"I don't want you to take her on your bicycle."

Wendy had come over to see Sally and was still in the apartment when Marcus got home. They all ate supper together, then Marcus and Wendy left.

At first it was nothing—Wendy telling him how much she liked Sally. His mother was the greatest, he agreed, but Wendy didn't have to live with her. Marcus was a little low, on an end-of-the-weekend downer. The weekend was gone, and what had he accomplished? Just as he'd

34

feared, the assignment for Sweeny still hung over him. As soon as he got Wendy home, he was going to knuckle down and do that work.

The chitchat died quickly. Wendy fell silent, and so did he.

"Here you are," he said, stopping front of her house. "Got you here in one piece."

"You're a good driver." Wendy looked around for her book and checked to see if the photos Sally had given her were inside. "Did you see these?" She handed the photos to Marcus. There were snapshots of Wendy and Grace, of Sally and Marcus, and one that embarrassed him of Wendy and him standing by a swing. He must have been ten or eleven then, in his fat phase. He had his shirt off and you could see the fat around his breasts—two tiny breasts like a girl's. He wished she didn't have that photo, but he handed it back without comment.

"Thanks for the ride," Wendy said, opening the door, but then she just sat there. "I hate going in," she said. "They're watching television. I can see the light. I always feel in the way."

"I thought you liked your aunt?"

"I do, I love her, and she's very good to me." Wendy let the door shut. "They always ask me to come and sit with them, but they're perfectly happy being alone. I never realized how lonely it would be living away from home. Even though I can't live with my mother, I miss her. Are you ever lonely, Marcus? Probably not. You have so many friends."

"Not lonely, exactly," Marcus said. There were moments when he sensed the loneliness at the edge of everything.

Without knowing exactly why, he'd always connected it to growing up without his father. "There are things I don't say to anybody."

"That's the lonely part isn't it?" Wendy said. "The things you keep to yourself." They sat in silence. "Wouldn't it be wonderful," Wendy said after a moment, "if we could be the kind of friends who can say anything to each other? Do you think we could, Marcus?"

At that moment he thought so. "Yes," he said. The things they were talking about surprised him. Real feelings. It touched him, and he felt very close to her.

When he got home he thought he would work. Sally was asleep, the apartment was dark: it was a perfect time. But instead of working he went up on the roof, and smoked his pipe, and looked up at the sky. Later he sat in the kitchen reading the *National Lampoon*, and eating leftover lamb stew.

He woke the next morning with a sinking feeling in the pit of his stomach. Sweeny's assignment due today, and he hadn't written a word. He groaned. He was a born-in-the-flesh procrastinator: everything put off for tomorrow. Well, there was no tomorrow. Sweeny waited. It was today or die.

It was still early. He jumped up, found his notebook, and got back in bed. Think about a character, a sincere, self-centered maniac who thought—no, who knew—he was the greatest, a guy without doubts, or questions, or uncertainties. Vic. Victor Gorman. *Good.*

He wrote it down. How would Victor be with someone like Bev Kruger? Marcus just had to think girl and King George was awake. Old Faithful . . . Old Reliable . . . Old Stupid.

Work, he ordered himself. Act your age. You've got an assignment to do. You're too old for this kind of stuff but it just felt too good. Oh, god, oh god . . . oh spit . . . oh damn. . . .

He came back to earth, aware of the antiseptic smell, the warmth, the slackness in his belly. Out of bed, muttering to himself, he changed everything. Seventeen, and still jerking off like a maniac. He wasn't proud of it. Procrastinator. Masturbator. Everything wrong with him had a Latin name, like a disease. Couldn't get a girl. What was the Latin word for that?

He thought about the piece for Sweeny all the way to school, then started writing in homeroom.

"Hail, Rosenbloom!" Gordy dropped his books on Marcus's desk like a bombshell. "What're you doing?"

Marcus grunted. He kept trying to work, but it was impossible. During first period trig he couldn't do a thing, and after class he grabbed Gordy by his tie and pulled his clever custardy face close to his "Tell Bastido I can't come to chem lab. Tell him I'm sick. If he wants to check on me, I'll be in the john."

Gordy adjusted his tie. "Really sick? Or malingering, as usual?"

Malingering: more Latin. "I'll be in the john till Sweeny's assignment is done."

He found a stall and jammed the door shut with his knees. This was the only place to write: a tiny space, uninteresting, colorless walls, a door he could lock, nobody to talk to or see. People came and went. The john filled with smoke, toilets flushed, doors banged, guys yelled.

At lunchtime his friends came looking for him. "Marcus?

37

Marcus Aurelius Rosenbloom?" Alec called in a stagy bellow. "Is that you in there?"

"Maybe he got flushed away," Pfeff said.

Marcus stuck out his toe. "This is a study hall. Shut up!"

"What are you doing in there?"

"Laying eggs. What do you think? Working."

"Genius at work," Gordy said. "Aren't you going to eat, genius?"

"Bring me two milks, an energy bar, and a couple of Hostess Twinkies."

Right on time he walked into Sweeny's class and handed him five closely written pages, scratched out in places and a little wrinkled. "That's it," Marcus said, smoothing out the pages. "Are you going to read it now?"

"Now?"

"Well . . . after class."

"I'll get to it as soon as I can, Mr. Rosenbloom."

Marcus caught Bev Kruger's eye and winked, then sat opposite her, swinging his leg, feeling irresistible, full of genius, love, and lust. "Bev, now that I've written a masterpiece, you and I ought to do something to celebrate."

Bev wrinkled her nose. "I don't think I'd like your idea of a celebration."

"Bev!" He put his hand to his heart. "I am sincere." He tried to make his eyes say, *I love you madly, I love you passionately.* Oh, he did love Bev, loved that lush garden of a body.

The class started. The fire inside Marcus didn't simmer down. Every time Sweeny said something, Marcus had a comment, a remark, a question. He was in his fast-talking, trigger-mouthed mood. "The creative process," he announced, "is sexual. Sex sublimated." At another point he said, "The creator has to believe in himself. Do you think God had doubts?" And it didn't stop there. After class he followed Bev from the room, still talking, as high as if he'd been drinking.

"I could follow you forever," he said at her shoulder, enthralled by the way her red jumper outlined her figure. He had the urge to bite her bare freckled arms. He felt the way he did when he stood on top of a building and had the urge to step off. He was going to do it. He bent toward her. She leaned away. "Let's speak of love and passion," he said. "Let's squeeze into your locker together and see what happens."

"Go bother somebody else, will you?" Her freckles blazed. "What's the matter with you today?"

He had to stop. He'd gone too far. He was sailing off across the waters and she was still sitting on the shore. Stop! he told himself, and he stopped—almost. "Farewell, lovely Beverly," he said, and with a lingering backward glance he strode down the hall whistling the Colonel Bogie march through his teeth.

6

Marcus caught sight of Wendy outside school. "Hey, Wendy!" She waved but kept walking, and he had to run to catch up. It was Wednesday, and he hadn't seen her since Sunday night when he'd driven her home, but the talk, the warmth had stayed with him. Something had been established, a layer of suspicion had been peeled away. They were solidly friends.

"Hey, Wendy, wait up."

"Your friend, Alec!" she burst out. "He walked right by me in the hall as if I was invisible."

"When?"

"Today, just a little while ago, outside the biology room."

"He must have been thinking about something."

"I was as close as I am to you!"

"He has trouble seeing sometimes."

"Come on, Marcus, he just forgot who I was."

"Oh, no, he was asking me all about you. How I knew you? Where you were from?"

"What'd you say?"

"I told him you were my friend."

"Your invisible friend."

"I told him I've known you a long time."

Wendy made a face. "I don't believe it. You're just being nice to me."

"It's true," Marcus said. "I didn't make it up." But what he didn't say were some of the other things Alec had said. He had guessed Wendy was the one Marcus had fallen on. "Go after it," Alec said. "That's stuff." Marcus had insisted that he and Wendy were friends, but Alec said there was no such thing between male and female. "They're either relatives or they're stuff." Marcus wasn't going to say that to Wendy.

He felt like saying, Don't get your hopes up. But why should he? Let Alec say it. Why should he make excuses for Alec? "What do you say to a Baskin-Robbins and some talk," he said, changing the subject. "Do you have time?"

She nodded and managed a smile. "I'm doing supper for my aunt, but I've got at least an hour free."

In the mall they sat on a bench eating their ice-cream cones, watching people pass in their bulky winter coats. "They look so tired," Wendy said. "Look at those mannikins, in the summer outfits, then look at the people. People can be so sad."

Marcus nodded, but his mind was elsewhere. He was

remembering the way he'd acted Monday when he'd handed in his paper to Sweeny, carrying on like an ass, raving about what an incredible piece of writing he'd done. Three days had passed and Sweeny hadn't said a word. He knew just what Sweeny was going to say when he handed him back his paper. Rosenbloom, he'd say, a flea's ass has more talent than you.

He was a blowhard! Telling everybody he was a writer, walking around with a notebook sticking out of his pocket. How could he be a writer? Where did he get the nerve to say he was anything? If he said he was a writer because he kept a notebook, than he could also say he was a lawyer because he liked to argue, or a doctor because he pulled splinters out of his skin.

"What's the matter, Marcus?"

"I'm worried about the paper I handed in to Sweeny."

"I'm sure it's good."

"You haven't read it," he said gloomily.

"Oh, what's the matter with us?" Wendy nudged him. "These gloom sessions. I think sometimes we just love groveling in the gloom."

"Do the grovel," Marcus said. He snapped his fingers. "When you're blue and out of sorts, do the grovel." He snapped his fingers, then took a bite out of the bottom of his cone.

"You're in trouble now," Wendy said. "It's all going to come out the bottom."

"That's life," Marcus said. "The bottom's always falling out."

"But keep smiling," Wendy said.

"Hang in there," Marcus said. The cliches were flying

thick and fast. "Don't let trouble get you down."

"Every cloud has its silver lining."

"Smile," Marcus said, and Wendy smiled. "Cry"—Wendy pulled down the corners of her mouth—"and you cry alone."

"It's been beautiful," Wendy said getting up. "I have to go."

"I'll walk with you." Strange things were happening. They were talking, he was enjoying himself, and he wasn't thinking about sex every second. Sometimes he felt his preoccupation with sex distorted his life. He didn't want to be looking at a girl's breasts all the time, but that's where his eyes led him. If he caught a glimpse of skin, his heart jumped. Even sex jokes he thought were stupid got a response from him that he couldn't control.

"What should we talk about now?" Wendy said. "We've covered the sad world."

"And cliches," Marcus said.

"And how good Alec's memory is. Almost as good as his eyesight. Oh, I don't know why it bothers me. I suppose I'm not the sort of girl guys remember."

"Here come the glooms." Marcus snapped his fingers. "Time to do the grovel."

Wendy struck herself. "Oh, no, am I doing it again? Let's talk about something cheerful, like sex."

"What's cheerful about that?"

"You sound like a jaded old pervert. Tell me what kind of girl Alec likes?"

"Big, blond, and California."

"Great, that leaves me out."

"There's nothing wrong with your looks."

"Thanks, friend. Marcus, when you look at a girl, what do you notice? What do you like particularly? Personality? Sense of humor? What?"

"What is this? TV? 'The Marriage Game'?"

"Answer the question."

"Knees," he said.

"Knees! I should have known. You *are* a pervert. Do you like my knees? On a scale of one to ten, how do my knees rate?"

"I can't really tell with those jeans on."

"I can't take them off here, sweetie. Oh, you're blushing. I made you blush."

Was he blushing? His hand went to his cheek. He hadn't meant to blush. "Boys don't blush," he said. "Girls blush, Barrett. Boys merely redden."

"Seriously, Marcus, what do you like in girls?"

"The three B's: bones, boobs, and butts."

"You guys are all alike. Such an emphasis on parts, as if you were talking about a car. 'Great headlights!' 'Great taillights!' 'Great bumpers!' Now if you asked me what I liked in a guy, I wouldn't talk about his separate parts. What I respond to is the total person."

"So what do you like about Alec?"

"Oh, I like his eyes."

"Come on, Wendy, more details, or I kick you off the panel."

"Well, I admit I noticed he had a cute tush."

"No separate parts, huh?"

They looked at each other and smiled. "Do you have fantasies about girls?" Wendy said. "I'm really curious about the kinds of things guys think of."

44

"You sound like a sociologist. Sure I have fantasies. Not like yours, though."

"What makes you think you know what goes on in my head?"

"Put that way, I take it back." But he couldn't believe anyone else could dream up some of the stuff that he did.

"I suppose your disgusting fantasies make you horny?" she said.

Marcus felt himself redden again. He didn't know how much experience Wendy had had, but from the way she talked, he had the feeling she *was* experienced. When had he ever talked to a girl like this before? He might have been talking to Alec, except that he'd never even described his fantasies to Alec. "My fantasies are off limits," he said. "Strictly confidential. Not for public consumption."

"Oh, come on," she coaxed. "What could my friend tell me that I wouldn't understand?"

"You'd be surprised. I have a nasty, low-down imagination."

"Here's another question for the panel. Are you hung up on a girl being a virgin?"

So his guess was right. She wasn't a virgin, and wanted him to know that interesting detail.

"Or do you think girls should have experience?"

"Either way," he said, more embarrassed than he wanted to show. "Just give me a girl." Now that was smart. That showed real intelligence.

"What about the girls you've gone out with?"

"Come on, knock it off." Was she going to get out her scorecard now, and regale him with her triumphs?"

"What's the matter?" Wendy said.

"Nothing!" He wasn't enjoying this. Now girls were bragging about how they'd scored.

"I can't understand why you're getting so mad. Did I say something? I know I talk too much. Am I talking too much?"

"Look—" and then at a loss for what to say, wanting to end it, but feeling himself getting in deeper and deeper, he said, "I haven't had that much experience." That should settle it. Let her think what she wanted.

"But you've had some?"

"Not that much," he said grudgingly.

"Well, how much?"

"How much have you had?"

"It's personal," she said.

"Same here."

Wendy looked at him. "We're both scared to say, aren't we?"

"I don't know what you're talking about."

"Well, I'll say it. My experience is zilch. Don't look so shocked, Marcus. Things don't happen in Buffalo the way they do everywhere else. I've made out. You're not impressed. I'm not either."

"Buffalo isn't the only place that's a desert," he said. She got the meaning right away.

"Truthfully?"

"Why is it so hard to believe? You think every guy's an expert?"

"I don't know. Just, *you* guys, I sort of thought . . . I look at guys and I think they all know. Alec comes on so, you know, sophisticated." She laughed.

"It so happens that Alec *is* sophisticated, if you know what I mean."

46

"Well, here we are." They were at her house. Did she catch that about Alec's sophistication?

"Sex isn't all that important," she said. "Don't misunderstand me, I know it is, but there's more to it than just sex. I've had my chances—not that many, but the guys made me mad, they were so stupid about it. You need someone special, don't you think so? Someone really close. Sometimes I feel I'll never find that person, and that's sad."

"You will," Marcus said. "I think if you want something enough it will happen." Then why hadn't it happened to him?

"I'd like to believe that everything turns out right in the end, but it doesn't for everyone." She was being serious again. "There's a loneliness in some people."

"You'll find someone," Marcus said. "It's going to happen to you. It happens to everyone." Kindly Dr. Fraud. "If I say any more I'll have to charge you, and sexologists don't come cheap."

"What I felt in the mall. Some people are sad all their lives. They cover up, but it's always there. In my sane moods I know that's why my mother keeps running from man to man. Well, I'd better go. Thanks for talking to me, Marcus."

He turned down Allen, then up Euclid toward home. Talking to Wendy was a surprise a minute. She hardly seemed to register what he had revealed about himself, something he'd never told anyone in the world before. He'd admitted that he was a virgin. It wasn't the kind of news he passed out routinely.

7

"Ladies and gentlemen," Mr. Sweeny said, "I've gone through each of your papers at least twice. You've introduced me to a number of interesting characters. I didn't know we had so much character around." Sweeny's little joke. "I'll read first a section of Miss Kruger's paper—one of the best."

Marcus doodled ferociously at the edge of his paper. Which one was his? Where was it, top or bottom? Today Sweeny was starting off with the best papers, handing out his praise, saving the losers for last.

Bev had written about her sister who had scoliosis, curvature of the spine, and who was in a full body cast. "Gayle has spent the last six months in the hospital," Sweeny read. "She does homework every day and delivers the newspapers to the other patients even though she is flat on her back. Her whole head is wrapped in bandages. She got tired of people thinking she was a boy, so she made a sign for the cart she wheels herself around on. The sign says, 'Hey, you guys, I'm a girl!' "

As he listened, Marcus felt envious, because he had had nothing so good to write about, nothing as real. And ashamed too, because he'd never credited Bev with anything but being sexy.

"Miss Kruger has written about a subject she knows. She has used good detail. She has us caring about her sister." High praise. Marcus sank down in his seat.

Mr. Sweeny went on to say something about several other papers. One belonged to a girl named Helen Wing. "Miss Wing wrote about her cousin Bovis, a lady who loves to fish and talks like a truck driver, if that's the way truck drivers still talk. Mr. Katz, your paper was also very good. Your aunt sounds like an interesting person."

Marcus returned to his scribbling, working the pen back and forth so hard it went through the paper. It was all downhill from here. In his despair he decided that Sweeny knew nothing about writing. Why should Marcus even listen to him? Whatever Sweeny said, it wasn't going to influence him.

Sweeny discussed each paper, taking his time, walking around the room, handing the paper back as he finished with it. Marcus knew his paper was on the bottom of the pile, so far down Sweeny couldn't even find it.

"Now I want to read you the last paper. What the author of this paper has done is create an interesting amalgam of truth and fiction, a melding of the memorable character with a person you really come to feel something for in an odd sort of way. Victor Gorman is self-centered, egotistical, not terribly bright, but so utterly sincere. Perhaps that's the clue." He picked up Marcus's paper. Marcus wanted to get up and leave the room. His stomach felt watery. He didn't want to listen to this.

"'Hey, I bet you think I talk a lot about myself,'" Mr. Sweeny read. The sound of his own words sent a shiver of fear down Marcus's back. But, god, it was good to hear his own words being read as if they mattered. "'A lot of people say, hey, that Victor Gorman has a very big head . . .'"

Was it good? Had he written that? The class was laughing. Was it funny? What were they laughing at?

"'I know people talk behind my back. People are very jealous of success and I have been very successful with the ladies. . . .'"

Did they know it was his? Maybe it *was* good.

Outside, at the end of the class, Marcus tried to read Sweeny's scrawl at the bottom of his paper. "If you are willing to work, this may be publishable. See me for a conference."

Publishable—to be published. To have his name in print. It was something he'd dreamed about, but to be taken seriously . . . It was real and it was unreal. What Sweeny had written both scared and excited him. Marcus told everyone he was a writer, but underneath, he didn't know what he was. He looked around for someone to tell, saw

Wendy through the library window, and went in. He dropped into the seat next to her and pushed the paper with Sweeny's comment toward her.

" 'This may be publishable,' " she read. "That's wonderful, Marcus. I bet you're walking on air."

"Sweeny's gone overboard."

"No, he hasn't. Read what Sweeny's said. It's good. You said yourself you thought it was good. Sweeny read it and knew."

"There's a lot of work to be done yet," the author said modestly.

"Where do you think you'll publish it?"

"*Playboy.*"

"You don't read *Playboy,* do you?"

Marcus took his story from her. "Do you think I would look at those filthy pictures?"

"Oh, Marcus, you lie so adorably. Wouldn't it be a riot, though, if they published your story?"

His mind took a leap: the editorial offices of *Playboy* . . . beautiful women . . . a telephone call from Hefner . . . invitation to the promising new writer . . . a swim in the *Playboy* pool . . .

"They'll probably throw me out of school, but I'd quit first. Actually I'm thinking about it: quitting school and just writing." He took a ballpoint pen and stuck it into the corner of his mouth. Marcus Rosenbloom Hemingway.

"It would take guts to do that," Wendy said, "to believe in yourself that much."

"I know it," he said. Something had happened that he hadn't fully absorbed yet. Somebody—no, Sweeny—had read what he'd written and said "what you have written is publishable." It meant that what he wrote was of interest to other people. It meant that he should write more.

"I'm going to write," he said to Wendy. His whole life would be reorganized around writing. No more screwing around panting after girls, wasting his life. He had purpose. School was irrelevant, the courses he was taking, trig, chemistry, even the diploma—all irrelevant. "If you know where you're going you go there. Everything else is irrelevant."

The idea grew as he talked. If his mother put up too much of a fuss, he'd leave home. He only needed a room to sleep and write in. He'd get a job as a counterman, a dishwasher; he'd live as simply as a grocery clerk. In his mind he'd already moved out. He was independent, working and writing. Everything would fall into place. Women would flock around him, the struggling genius.

It was only when he was alone that his feet touched the ground. He was being carried away. Would *Playboy* take his piece? Did he dare leave school? But despite everything, the idea stuck.

"You know the paper I had to do for Sweeny?" Marcus met his mother downtown for supper and told her what Sweeny had said, and what he had written on the bottom of his paper. "What do you think of that?"

Sally sipped her soup. "I think it's wonderful. You must have gotten an A on that paper."

Wasn't that like his mother not to get the point. "The A is irrelevant." He paused, took a swallow of water. "It's more than an A. I should be writing more, not wasting my time in school."

"You are writing. You're taking an interesting course.

You were so enthusiastic about your teacher."

"Sweeny's great, but he's only one teacher." He was anxious for her approval and resentful that he needed it. "I'm ready to drop out."

That stopped her eating. "I can't believe you're serious. You've always liked school."

"I'm going to write every day," he said. "Every day, all day."

"Write all day? Be realistic," Sally said. "It's impossible for you to sit still for thirty seconds."

"Jesus." Couldn't she see him as anything but a snotty, squirmy kid? "I want to get started on my life, can't you understand?"

"You keep talking about life," his mother said, "as if it's something that only you know anything about. Don't you think I know a little about life?"

"No comment," Marcus said.

"Marcus, only three more months and you graduate. Then college, that's the next step. You can't go anyplace in the world of work without those diplomas."

"College. Is that the only thing left to do in the world? Where's adventure? Where's just sailing out and seeing where you land? What about going out and getting my lumps and finding out if I can take it or not? Look, Sally—" He could see she wasn't getting it, and he was beginning to bounce up and down. Calm down, he told himself, act normal. He tasted his soup. "How's your soup, Sally?" He spoke softly. "Mine's delicious." He tasted a spoonful. "I want to talk about this calmly. Writing is work, Sally. I'm not leaving school to bum around. I'm going to be working night and day."

"A writer needs a lot of talent."

"And you don't think I have enough to fill an ant's hole!" He pushed the soup away, spilling it.

"Look, control yourself."

"What the hell, will you stop treating me like a freaking baby and talk?"

Sally reached for her purse. "I'm leaving," she said. "I'm not going to talk to you the way you're acting."

"Are you going to walk out on me?" He was whispering. Control, that's what he needed, control. "I don't want you to walk out on me. I want to settle this, now!"

She was mad, he could see how mad she was. "I didn't say you shouldn't think about being a writer. Yes, you need talent. And one high-school paper is not enough! You don't become a writer because you say so."

He slapped the table. "It's more than one paper. I've had things in the school magazine this year, and last year, and the year before." He was pumping things up. Sure he'd had pieces printed, but anyone could get into that ratty magazine. But Sally's opposition only redoubled his desire to win. The idea of quitting school was just building in him. He didn't want her telling him anything. It was *his* life. If he was making a mistake, it was his mistake. He'd suffer for it, not her.

"I can't take this seriously. This is your last term. You're so close to graduation. To throw it all up now—you can't be serious." She was starting all over again.

"Okay!" he said, "Okay, folks, she's finally done it! My mother has finally done it, folks! Driven me bug-eyed crazy mad! Okay, Sally, you think it's a joke? You think *I'm* a joke. Right! It is a joke. I was just testing you, seeing if your reflexes were still intact. That's right I'm not going

54

to be a writer. I'm going to get a job on a garbage truck."
He was on his feet. "Let the world hear. A joke—I'm a
joke too, but I'm through with high school. I'm not going
back, Sally. That's no joke. I've stopped talking." And
he walked out.

But did anything ever end with his mother? "All right,
let's talk seriously," she said later, "see if we can work
out something." Why couldn't they meet halfway, she said.
Compromise. She was willing to give, so he should be,
too. "For instance, why don't you rearrange your schedule.
Drop the course you don't need, keep the ones you do
need. Can't you take the classes you need in the morning,
say, then have your afternoons free for writing?"

Halfway measures: that was Sally. But in a way he was
relieved. She was satisfied, and for the time being so was
he.

The schedule turned out to be a lot easier to arrange
than he'd imagined. He didn't need trig for graduation.
He dropped gym with the proviso that he'd swim at the
school pool two times a week. It was all set. He could
leave before lunch every day, and Sweeny agreed to give
him a conference once a week on Thursdays.

He had been dreaming, and then he'd been fighting with
his mother, and now he'd done it. Now there was no turning back. He was going to have to write half a day, every
day, whether he had anything to write or not.

8

In preparation for his career as a writer, Marcus cleaned his room. It was important that everything be right. A portable typewriter was on the desk. Next to the lamp he had a mason jar with pens and pencils, a Webster's dictionary, and *Roget's Thesaurus*. The Victor Gorman story was in a folder in the top drawer, his notebooks in the second drawer, and in the bottom drawer a fresh ream of paper.

Monday morning, the first day of his new schedule, he woke early. He heard the hum of traffic, a door slam, the exciting sound of a woman's heels in the hall. Life! He felt like springing straight up—Shazam!—up through the roof.

All morning in school he kept getting these intense feelings about himself, and life. At noontime, accompanied by his friends, he walked out. Alec and Gordy had their arms locked through his, and Pfeff was saying they ought to get the school photographers and make a media event of it. Marcus saw Wendy and she came along. "What's going on?" she said, and glanced at Alec.

"I'm leaving today," Marcus said. "Come say good-bye." He shook hands with everyone. "I'm going to miss you guys." He started getting sentimental.

"Yeah, we're going to miss you too," Pfeff said, "like a mosquito bite."

"This is a solemn moment," Alec said. He looked at Wendy. "Just a few words of farewell to our comrade Marcus Aurelius Rosenbloom, who today begins a new life."

Marcus rolled his eyes and made Wendy laugh.

"It takes courage to dedicate yourself to art. We want Marcus to know we admire what he's doing, and as a token of our love, we have pooled our resources for this gift that I know he will put to good use. Gordy, the appreciation gift?"

Marcus opened a package hastily wrapped in what looked suspiciously like toilet paper. "A Bic ballpoint pen." He held it up for everyone to see. "You shouldn't have."

"Speech, speech," Wendy cried. Alec applauded.

"I don't know what to say," Marcus said.

Alec slapped him on the back. "That's perfect, Marcus, and beautifully put." He pushed open the door. "Go before the moment is ruined."

Outside the streets were quiet, clean, and empty. Marcus walked by rows of houses. There was order in the world:

57

parents working, kids in school. Only Marcus Rosenbloom, like a pebble in a shoe, was in the wrong place. Suddenly he couldn't think of any reason for doing what he'd done. *Please take me back, warden.* The prisoner was released after serving almost twelve years, given afternoons off for good behavior. *But I don't know how to live in the world, warden. I love it here in Sherwood Gaol. I swear I do.* What was he going to do with himself every afternoon? Where would he eat lunch? Who would he talk to? Writing, what was that?

All was quiet at home, deadly still. He sat at his desk, his pens lined up, a fresh sheet of paper in the typewriter. And then . . . and then. . . . Nothing. His mind was blank. *Write something.* He stared at the paper for a long time. Finally he typed out the argument he'd had with his mother in the restaurant. He was surprised when he looked at the clock how little time had passed.

All week in school, his friends kept asking how the writing was going. "How's it going, Hemingway?" Gordy said.

"Slow but sure," Marcus said. "Writing's not play, but it's coming." The same speech for Mr. Sweeny and his mother. "Writing's not play, but it's coming." He was quickly sick of hearing himself say it.

Every night when he heard his mother at the door, he'd sit at his desk a little longer so she'd know he was working hard. "Well," she'd say when he emerged, "How was it today?"

"Terrific," he'd say. "Yes, it started awful and ended horrible."

The rule was that he must sit at his desk for three hours

every day, the same three hours he would have spent in school. And no skips allowed. There he sat like a chicken on an egg waiting for something to hatch. He'd scribble a few notes, write a sentence, sit there for fifteen, sometimes twenty minutes, then give himself a break. Get up, stretch, yawn, wander into the kitchen, eat a piece of cheese, drink a glass of milk, check out the newspaper, flip on the TV, watch for a while, then take a leak.

By that time another fifteen, twenty, or twenty-five minutes had passed. Once in a while the phone rang. Someone selling ironing board covers. He clipped his nails, adjusted the shade at the window, waited for the phone to ring again.

Saturday morning he and Alec played tennis. "You look like a monkey on his way to Wimbledon," Marcus said, settling back in Alec's car. Alec was wearing white shorts, a white shirt with red piping, white socks with red stripes, and sneakers with red slashes. "A hairy monkey."

Alec took a look at Marcus's cutoffs, torn Adidas, and oversized Baltimore Colts shirt. "And you look like a refugee from the Salvation Army. So how's it feel doing nothing?"

"Like nothing." He was so phony. It was incredible what he was telling people and what he was really doing. He was as big an actor as Alec. But at least people knew when Alec was acting. They thought Marcus was telling the truth, and the truth was he felt dumb, he'd done so little this week. Practically nothing.

Alec checked his watch. "I've got a rehearsal this afternoon. Terri and I are doing the kissing scene."

Marcus began to see another serious flaw in the writer's

life: no women. "How's the leading lady?"

"Gorgeous. Did you know your girl friend has been coming to rehearsal every day?"

"Girl friend?"

"Wendy. She's there almost every day. Just sits in back and watches."

Marcus felt a twinge of jealousy, but he admired Wendy's persistence. She wanted Alec and she was going after him. Just the way he was about being a writer. Did he really believe that? Well, it was only the first week, he'd hardly given himself a chance. Next week he'd really knuckle down. That made him feel better, and he started teasing Alec. "Are you sure you saw Wendy at rehearsal? I heard that your eyesight fails you sometimes."

"It was Ranger Wendy, all right. I was close enough to tell." He smirked. "A very friendly person."

What did that mean? As if he didn't know.

On the tennis court, Marcus played aggressively, smashing the ball back at Alec, beating him three sets straight. "You play like an animal," Alec said, drying his face. "I should have been concentrating more. My game's a lot better than yours. I was off today."

"Your mouth sure isn't."

Things were not going well for Marcus. In three weeks at home, all he did was work on the Victor Gorman piece. Sweeny kept wanting him to do more. Marcus sat at his desk and made lists of the cans and dry goods in the cupboard, the contents of the medicine cabinet, the names and apartment numbers of everyone who lived in the building.

"How's it going, Marco?" Wendy said, meeting him in the hall in school.

"Writing's not play." He was afraid she'd start asking him what he was working on. *My fingernails, and when I'm done with them, I'll start on my toenails.* He rushed past her. Then he felt he had acted badly. When he saw her later he went up to her and said, as if they were in the middle of a conversation, "Well, when are we going to get together and do something?"

"When the train stops for the station." Wendy straightened her fatigue cap. "You know, you are hard to take sometimes, Rosenbloom."

"I'm up and down," he admitted. "But I've missed your cheerful mug." He liked the way she was dressed, her baggy fatigue pants, and the tight green T-shirt that said When God Made the World She Wasn't Kidding Around.

"I miss your happy face too," Wendy said.

"Come on over after school, and we'll get out and talk."

"I don't like taking you away from your work."

"No, no, that's all right." He didn't say that sometimes he felt like dragging people in off the streets for company.

Thursday, Sweeny handed Victor Gorman back to Marcus. "Send it out. I think it's as good as it's going to be."

"But is it good enough?" Marcus murmured. His mouth was dry. "Maybe I should work on it some more."

"Where's the Rosenbloom bravado? Submit it and see what happens."

"Okay, I'll send it to *Playboy*."

"Why not? Give it a try. Might as well start at the top."

At home Marcus typed up the final copy. He typed slowly, groaning every time his fingers hit the wrong key. Downstairs he dropped the yellow manila envelope into the mailbox, then leaned against it feeling a proprietary interest. No more mail in this box. Some fanatic might mail a bomb; you never could tell. He sternly eyed a kid who had a letter in her hand. "What kind of stuff you mailing?"

The girl looked at him. Marcus realized he was blocking the U.S. Mail and stepped aside. "You look like a good kid," he said. Walking away, the girl twirled her finger at her forehead. Marcus continued to stand by the mailbox, not quite as militantly as he had before, a little more relaxed—more as an interested friend of the mail service.

For a day his mood soared, but then he had to think of something new to write. He began to go out afternoons. The author in search of a story. He wore a long green wool scarf and a corduroy jacket with pockets for his notebook, pipe, and pens. He might be mistaken for an English writer. Thomas Hardy. No, he was dead. The great James Joyce. Should he buy a pair of steel-rimmed glasses?

He went flying around the city, his head full of fantasies, but in the end he knew clearly that he wasn't writing. A lot of little scribbles—"Bird droppings," he called them. He wasn't doing what he'd said he would do, write three hours a day. He was only playing at being a writer. Staying home had turned into a disaster.

Should he go back to school, admit he'd failed? Could he face Sweeny, and his friends, and his mother? Not after the show he'd put on for her! She'd said he couldn't sit still for thirty seconds. She was right and he was wrong. Better wait. *Playboy* was going to love his story. *That Rosenbloom, he's a gem in the rough.* Dreaming again, but still, he should wait till he heard from *Playboy* and then decide.

Meanwhile he applied for a stock clerk job at Nadia's, a neighborhood market. A man wearing a black toupee took Marcus's application. It was Nadia himself, sitting in a high booth. "Can you work evenings?"

"Yes, sir."

"Weekends?"

"Yes."

"Okay," Captain Nadia said, "we'll be in touch with you."

"Will it be soon, sir?"

"We'll be in touch with you." He was dismissed.

"Captain Birdbrain," Marcus muttered.

As he left the market he held the door for a tall, striking-looking woman with a little boy. "Do you know where I can put up a notice," she said? She thought he worked in the store. He pointed to the bulletin board inside the vestibule.

"Are there any tacks?"

He pried a tack from the board and pinned up her notice. She stood close to him. Smooth, almost silvery hair hung to her shoulders. Black crayon lines of mascara outlined her eyes. She had a long regal nose, the nose of a princess.

"There." She stood back and looked at her notice. "I hope that will catch people's eyes." The notice was bordered with a design of red and yellow roses.

She picked up the little boy who had sat down on the floor. The woven silver bands around her wrist slid to her elbow. Then she pushed open the door—*she was leaving!* "A lot of people come through here," he said.

"Really." Total indifference. An Ice Princess.

He stood and watched her go, saw her get into a red Mustang and drive off. Then he moved, had to . . . didn't think . . . couldn't think. He ran down the street but it was too late. She had appeared out of nowhere and now she had disappeared again.

9

Thursday, Marcus had his weekly conference with Mr. Sweeny and had nothing to show him, just hoped he could fake it somehow. Mr. Sweeny was at his desk in the crowded office he shared with three other teachers. "Sit down, Marcus. How's it going?"

"Fine." Marcus put on a false smile of confidence. His hand went to his back pocket for his notebook.

"What have you got to show me?"

The notebook was open to a page of lists he'd made: what people had in their shopping baskets, the names of stores on a certain street, the names of people who had made the obituary page that week. He handed Sweeny the notebook. "My laundry lists."

Sweeny flipped the pages casually. "What's all this?"

"I like the names of things. Open your drawer. I'll copy down everything inside, or what you have in your pockets."

Sweeny handed him back the notebook. "All very interesting, but what does it mean?"

He should have known Sweeny wouldn't be taken in with his lists.

"What else have you been doing this week?"

"I'm working on something else." And then the tall woman he'd seen in the market yesterday came to his mind, and he thought of the way she had disappeared.

"Can I see what you're working on?"

"Well . . ." Marcus dug around in his pockets, found a pen. "I didn't bring it because it's not that developed yet." He was improvising. "It's about a girl."

"Tell me a little more."

"It's about"—he said the first thing that came into his head—"Isabel Malefsky."

"Isabel Malefsky." Sweeny nodded. "Good name for a character. I'm interested."

Marcus looked at the notebook in his hands. Isabel Malefsky was no character in a story. She'd been in his sixth-grade class, his first great obsession. He'd followed her around all one term like a dumb dog, and never spoken a word to her. He'd been a fat, crazy kid who couldn't talk to a girl.

"What's the story?" Sweeny said.

"It's developing, coming slowly. I'm not ready to talk about it yet." What a hypocrite. He could hardly wait to get away.

That afternoon he couldn't face his desk. The conference

with Sweeny—he didn't even want to think about it. Laundry lists! Disgusted with himself, he tossed the notebook aside. Maybe it would grow wings and fly away. Then he picked it up, afraid somebody would find it and read it. *Great! Look what the birds are dropping these days.* Sweeny should have laughed out loud. And then bringing up Isabel Malefsky. What was he possibly going to write about her? Where had she come from? He hadn't thought about her in years. Was it because of the tall woman yesterday? He sensed the same obsession he'd once felt for Isabel building in him again. In everything he did he felt the fanatic in himself. The way he got ideas in his head: nothing could wait. His desire to be a writer. The year he'd searched for his father; the man had hardly looked at him. Sally had warned him that time, too, but nobody could stop Marcus once he got an idea in his head. And was the tall woman only the latest fanatical idea? Yes, he wanted to see her again. And that afternoon he went back to Nadia's Market.

Her notice for a baby-sitter was still up. Then he'd wait till she came back. And what if she never came? Maybe she had put notices up in every store in the city. And if she did walk through these doors right now, what could he say to her? The answer was easy. *I'll take the baby-sitting job.* Without another thought he took down the notice and folded it into his pocket.

He called her from a street phone in front of the dry cleaners.

"Hello?" It was her.

"Uh, uh . . ." He didn't know her name. He was nervous, afraid now that someone else had answered the ad and taken the job. "This is me . . . the man . . . the fellow at the market."

"Who?"

"Marcus Rosenbloom. I got you the tack yesterday, to put up your notice."

"Oh, right." A long silence.

"Did somebody answer your ad?"

"No, not yet."

"Except me." She didn't get it.

"I really need somebody very soon. Do you happen to know anybody?"

"I'll work for you."

"You? No, I want a girl. Do you know a girl, or a woman?"

"I don't, no. But I'm looking for a job. I like kids."

She was silent then, for a minute. "I couldn't pay you enough. Besides, it's not a full-time job."

"I don't want a full-time job. I go to school mornings."

"No, I don't think so."

He closed his eyes, saw the silver bracelets slide down her arm. *What are you doing, Marcus? Stop.* But he was in the grip of those obsessive feelings and couldn't stop.

"Why don't you try me for a couple of days and see how I work out?"

"I never had a boy sitter before."

"I'm available now."

Silence. Then, as if she were thinking aloud, "I do need someone. Could you be here tomorrow at twelve-thirty?"

Yes, he could! She gave him her name and address. He repeated them: "Karen Lambert, Thurber Street."

"You understand, it's just for one day. If I find a girl?"

68

"For one day," he repeated, but felt as if he'd just won a wonderful prize.

Before he went to Karen Lambert's house the next day, Marcus showered and changed his shirt and jeans. At her house he carried the bike up on the porch, then blew into his hand. Breath okay. She lived in the upper story of a white, two-family house. Marcus climbed the steep narrow stairs. Besides his notebook he'd brought a book with him, *The Web and the Rock* by Thomas Wolfe. A big book, a thick book, a serious book. He was a serious reader, a student, a writer, not an irresponsible kid.

"Mark?"

"Marcus," he said. "Marcus Rosenbloom."

She opened the door and looked down as if she were doubting the wisdom of letting him come any farther. Standing above him, she seemed taller than he remembered, tall and narrow, almost fragile, with narrow bony shoulders and thin ankles that aroused the most intense feelings in him. He felt helpless beneath her dark-fringed eyes, sure that she didn't trust him, had changed her mind. She was going to send him away.

He held up the book, a medallion, proof of his sincere intentions. "Am I late?"

"Where do you live?" she demanded.

He gave his address.

"You go to school?"

"Yes, mornings."

"What school?"

He told her.

"Why only mornings?"

"I, uh, I'm doing independent studies. Writing."

69

"What does your father do?"

"I live with my mother. She works at the State Employment Building." He didn't know at what moment she was reassured, but she finally let him pass. She glanced at her watch, then picked up her son. "Kevin, do you remember this boy from the market?"

The child regarded him solemnly.

"I've written out instructions for you," she said to Marcus. "Here's the phone number of the Everson. I'm a curator there. If you have any trouble, read the instructions. If it's something you can't handle, call me. I'll be back between five-thirty and six." She put Kevin down. "Honey, you be good. Remember, I told you Marcus was going to play with you."

"Nooo," Kevin cried.

"Sweetheart—" She looked at her watch, then kissed Kevin. "I have to go, honey."

Afterward Kevin stood stolidly at the door. "Let's play," Marcus said. Kevin shook his head.

Marcus looked around the room, at the half-empty packing boxes, the stereo on the floor, the paintings stacked against the wall. It looked like she'd just moved in. What had he let himself in for? Who was she? It had started when he saw her in the market, and now here he was, the baby-sitter. He looked at his instructions.

"Kevin has had his lunch . . . he'll be thirsty . . . prefers o.j., but try to get him to take milk . . . can have crackers . . . no cookies, please . . ." There was a page of instructions: what to do when Kevin got tired, where to call if he hurt himself, what blankets he liked in his bed.

"How about some milk and a cracker, Kevin?" He went

into the kitchen, poured a glass of milk. What do you say to a kid? "Look what I've got. Hey, boy, this stuff is terrific." He held out the milk. Kevin put his hands behind his back. Marcus drank a little. "Good!" He rubbed his stomach. "Mmm, makes me strong." He made a muscle. Kevin watched. Marcus took another sip. "Want to share?" Kevin shook his head. "Tell you what, I'll drink milk today, and you"—Marcus pointed dramatically at the small boy—"you, Kevin Lambert, you lucky, fortunate fellow can have *orange juice.*"

He had to keep inventing things. When they sat on the rug it was a boat, their supplies the crackers and orange juice. That's the way the afternoon went. Marcus made up a story about two Meows and an Ouch who lived under the rug. He kept racking his brain for more games and stories to keep Kevin happy. Finally Kevin fell asleep in his arms as he was telling him a story.

Afraid he'd wake, Marcus left the boy there, but eased into a more comfortable position on the rug, then looked around. She had a painting of a Maxwell House coffee can, a big red plastic stuffed heart, an old-fashioned, yellowing wedding gown hanging from a light fixture, and, suspended from a hook in the ceiling, a mobile made of curls of silver foil. Everywhere he felt her presence. Everything he saw aroused that tightness in his center somewhere between his heart and his groin.

Karen was home earlier than he expected. She caught him by surprise, rushing in and snatching up Kevin. Her face was full of color. He hardly dared look at her, she was so beautiful.

"Did everything go all right?" She looked around, check-

71

ing everything in the room, as if she didn't trust him.

"Fine, fine, fine, great. Kevin and I had a great time, didn't we, Kevin old buddy?" Blabbing on: he could hardly stop himself.

"Did Kevin get his nap?" With Kevin on one arm, she fished in her purse for money. He thought, She can't wait to get rid of me.

He looked around for his book. This was it. She would pay him and tell him not to bother returning.

"I sleep," Kevin confirmed. "Mommy, Mommy, under the rug, two meows and a bark."

Marcus reddened. "It's a story I told him."

She handed him the money. "What about tomorrow?"

"Tomorrow?" he said, confused.

"Can you come again tomorrow?"

"Do you want me to?"

"Yes, if you're available. You do want the job?"

"Yes, sure, if you want me."

"If it's all right, I'll pay you each day. Let's go along this way and see how things work out."

"I'll be here," he said. He was so elated he practically flew down the stairs.

On the way home he began to worry about what he was going to say to his mother. *"Sally, I have a baby-sitting job." "You're baby-sitting!"* He could just hear the way she'd say it. *"Is that why you left school?"*

And what could he say? Tell her it wasn't the baby-sitting job, it was Karen? Never! He wouldn't discuss Karen with his mother or anyone else.

Then why *was* he baby-sitting? *To know more about the younger generation. Children are an important step in*

72

the life process. Ugh! It would be just like him to make a pompous ass statement like that. But what *was* he going to tell his mother? Nothing. And put *that* off as long as possible.

He was starved when he got home. To his surprise Wendy was there waiting for him. She followed him into the kitchen. "You invite me over and then you're not here."

"Well, here I am." He looked on the stove, then in the refrigerator. "You want to eat?"

"Is that you, Marcus?" Sally called from the bathroom. "I'm going to take a shower."

"I want to talk to you," Wendy said.

"Talk," Marcus said. He threw a package of frozen lasagna into a pan, then turned up the heat. "Do you want some of this?"

"What is it?"

"Cheese lasagna."

"I don't know." Wendy peered into the hall, then came back. "Are we private here?"

"Do you mean is Sally listening?"

"I don't want anyone else to hear this. It's about Alec and me."

Marcus spooned yogurt on a piece of bread, then added a green scallion. "I thought you two were going great guns?"

"Who said so?"

"Alec. Who else?" Marcus started to take a bite, but Wendy pulled his hand away.

"He did? What did he say exactly?"

"He said you were coming to rehearsals and you were very friendly."

"What does that mean!" Wendy frowned at the sandwich

Marcus was about to taste. He offered it to her but she shook her head. "Friendly? I suppose that's because we talk. Alec likes to talk."

"You can say that again." Marcus bit into the bread. Yogurt spurted over his fingers.

"Marcus, I can't talk to you when you're eating."

He licked his fingers, then sat up on the counter. "Okay, talk fast. I'm hungry."

"The thing is . . ." Wendy twisted the chain around her neck. "Alec and I have been making out and—"

"Stop right there! I don't want to hear about it. These confessions give me a pain in the buttinski. I don't want to hear the sordid details."

"There are no sordid details. That's just the problem. Making out makes it sound a lot better than it was. We kissed a little—no, it was a lot—one night." Wendy's eyes shone. "It was fantastic. We sat there and talked till everyone left and they turned out the lights. We had the whole place to ourselves and he put his arm around me—Marcus, are you listening?"

He flipped the lasagna over and turned down the heat. "Sure." But he was thinking about Karen, the two of them alone in her apartment . . . Karen with her arms around his waist . . . so crazy for him she couldn't let him go . . .

"Do you know what I'm saying? Do you know what it means when someone you like likes you?"

"Of course I do." But did he? Of all the girls he'd ever liked, had one of them ever fallen for him the way Wendy had for Alec?

"I was in a daze, Marcus. Something started that night. The way I felt, it had to go someplace. I knew we were going to see each other again, and it was going to get better and better."

"What are you telling me for?"

"The point is that was the first and the last time. Since then we talk, but aside from that, nothing."

"Maybe you have bad breath. Here, blow and I'll tell you. What are friends for?"

"Marcus, I'm going to hit you if you don't stop joking. I'm not joking. It's not funny to me." She was upset. "You're the only person I can talk to."

"Sorry." Jokes. The worst part of him was making jokes about everything. With Alec, Pfeff, and the others, nothing was serious. The code was, nothing hurt. If you sat on a tack, you gave a hard-ass laugh. He looked at Wendy soberly. The Comforting Friend. There, he was making jokes again. The Embarrassed Adolescent. What was the matter with him? He did know how Wendy felt. Hadn't he just come from Karen's?

"Do you know how exciting that first night was? I would have done it right there on the stage if he'd wanted to."

"Wendy!" Marcus's hand went to his stomach. "I'm going to puke."

"It's the truth, Marcus. Alec is terribly exciting, at least to me."

Marcus grimaced.

"I'm talking too much, I know—" She broke off as Sally entered the room in a blue bathrobe, a towel wrapped around her hair like a turban.

"You came in late tonight, Marcus. Where were you?" Sally poured herself a glass of grapefruit juice. "I'm catching cold. I'm going to lie down. I'm sorry I'm not better company, Wendy."

"That's all right, Sally. I'm fine."

"Wendy came to see me, Mom, not you."

"Please," Sally said with a nervous gesture. "Not tonight." She went back to her room.

"I'm a mother's dream," Marcus said, mocking himself, relieved that he didn't have to talk to his mother tonight. He took the pan of lasagna from the stove and started eating, then, belatedly, he offered some to Wendy.

"No, I can't eat."

"Mind if I do?"

"Wait." She checked the kitchen door. "Don't eat yet. There's more to talk about. This thing with Alec, it's the story of my life. I meet a guy I like and he's not interested, or *if* he's interested, he's a turkey. Eighteen, and I'm still waiting. Do you know the pressure there is on girls? And it isn't only that. I want something to happen. For *me.* How long do I have to wait?"

"Let me consult my computer and I'll give you a precise date."

"I just want you to tell me one thing: is there somebody else? Alec said he wasn't going with anybody. Is that true?"

"As far as I know." Then he remembered Terri, but felt he couldn't say anything. He was torn, loyal to Alec, but loyal to Wendy too. "I don't know what goes on in Alec's head. He's always got a girl hanging around. You'd be better off if you got interested in someone else. Does it have to be Alec?"

"I didn't *decide* it," Wendy said. "You don't decide these things. It happened. Like lightning."

76

Like lightning. Like the first time he saw Karen. He was tempted to tell Wendy, but how could you compare Alec and Karen? Or the way he felt about Karen to the way Wendy felt about Alec?

"Marcus, I want you to find out if Alec is interested in somebody else so I can know where I stand. And for God's sake, don't say that I asked. Just find out. If Alec's not interested, I'm giving him up."

"Can you do that?"

"I will. Once I make up my mind to something, I can make myself do anything. Anyway, sometimes I think it's nothing but sex."

Was it sex that had attracted him to Karen?

"And if it's just sex—" She gave Marcus a tight little smile. "What if I picked up a guy and I said, 'How do you do, sir, you just won a lottery and the prize is me?' And off we'd go. I wouldn't tell him my real name. It would just be that one time. I'd do it and get it over with. Then maybe I wouldn't feel this way about every guy I like."

"You make it sound like a dose of medicine."

"I wish I could take it like medicine. Then I could relax and stop thinking about it so much."

"I know," Marcus said. Did he ever know! That's what he'd been saying all along: *Let me do it and get it over with*. But nobody was listening.

IO

As he expected, his mother didn't applaud when he told her about taking a baby-sitting job. She said things he didn't really want to hear. "You changed our agreement without consulting me. I don't understand why you've done this. Is it money you need? I'll be glad to discuss your allowance."

He winced, but he stood there and listened because there was no way his mother wasn't going to say her piece. Karen! He could never talk about her to Sally. He wanted . . . he wanted. . . . Nothing his mother said would make any difference.

Marcus was in love. Or was it lust? He couldn't make

up his mind. Where did love end and lust begin? Where did lust end and love begin? "Karen" . . . he said her name. She was perfect, she was different—those shell-like ears, that long regal nose. All his fantasies focused on Karen, in need, fragile, sensitive, helpless, turning to him. When he thought about her—about them, really, Marcus and Karen—everything was magnified and exaggerated. They were on a mountaintop, Karen raised in his arms, the sky behind them, the sun setting. And somewhere, hidden behind rocks, the voices of a thousand musicians. Pure Hollywood corn.

Those were his good fantasies. Then there were his bad, low-down, raunchy fantasies. Alone with Karen, and she, calling him into her room . . . Or waiting at the head of the stairs, her robe falling open . . .

Every day when he arrived at Karen's it was the same thing. "Oh, there you are," she'd say as if she were surprised to see him. And he'd raise his book in greeting, then give Kevin the dandelions he'd picked on the way, because he didn't have the nerve to give them to Karen.

She looked at him with a calm, mocking expression. He was sure she saw through him, what he dreamed and pretended. *What do you know?* she seemed to say. *What have you done? What can you do? Prove yourself.*

When he was alone he studied his face in the mirror, wondering what she thought of him. Sometimes he knew he was good-looking. Sometimes he hated his smooth skin. When he got depressed, he thought he looked like a fat white egg.

Karen was always friendly enough, but cool, the way you would act with a baby-sitter. She was paying, so she could have things exactly the way she wanted. *Even me*, he thought, and fantasy . . . her robe loosening . . . leaped up again.

Despite her coolness, he lived for the moment when he was taking the stairs two at a time. "Oh, it's you," she said. "I'll be late today. Could you give Kevin supper? Make him a hamburger. Do you cook?"

"Do I cook?" Near her he was always acting, not himself, trying to impress her. "I'm a fantastic cook!"

She gave him one of her infrequent smiles. "I know, you guys can do anything these days."

"I cook for my mother all the time." Why had he said that? Doing things for his mother like a kid. He was sensitive to the difference in their ages. She was somewhere in her mid-twenties. If she asked, he planned to say he was already eighteen, maybe nineteen. Let her think he was a little retarded in school. I lost a year, he'd tell her. I had mono, the lover's disease.

The job became routine. He played with Kevin, read to him, invented stories. Sometimes they sang songs. "Old McDonald Had a Farm" was Kevin's favorite. Every time they sang it they had to sing it all the way through, and not just once, but two or three times. It drove Marcus crazy. When Kevin took his nap, Marcus wrote in his notebook. Now that he had less time to write, he was writing more than before. He was working on the Isabel Malefsky story he had promised Sweeny. Someday he would show Karen his work, let her read it, prove to her that he was a writer, as much an artist as she was.

It would start with talk—a little talk, a little touching, her fingers light on his arm. *Marcus.* She'd breathe his name . . .

"Love," he wrote, "lust, what men feel for women: primal, earthy, unmistakable, like hunger, cold, thirst. Love is a corrupted word. I love my mother. I'd love a new car. I love to beat Alec at tennis. None of these things is what I feel for Karen."

But when he tried to write what he really felt about her, all that came to his mind were canned words, phrases from ads or songs: *silvery hair . . . eyes like moonlight . . . lady, my lady.* Not his words; other people's words.

He sat with his notebook on his knees. "Karen," he wrote. "Karen . . . Karen. . . ."

One afternoon, while Kevin slept, Wendy came over. Marcus showed her everything in the apartment: the books, the sculptures, the wedding dress. Karen's bedroom door was ajar, and they looked in. The dim room, the crumpled sheets, the blankets half on the floor filled him with excitement.

In the hall Wendy studied a series of drawings of male nudes. "Great bods," she said. "It's really a different place. What's she like?"

He gestured around the apartment. "You can see."

Wendy examined a hanging made of bark, leaves, and feathers. "Did you talk to Alec?"

"I haven't forgotten," he said quickly. "I just haven't had a chance." Why was he so uncomfortable? Why was he making excuses? He had tried. A couple of times he'd dropped Wendy's name into the conversation, but Alec hadn't bitten. Marcus was sorry now that he'd agreed so readily to speak to Alec. He was afraid what Alec would say wouldn't be what Wendy wanted to hear, and he didn't want to be the messenger with the bad news. He knew Alec a lot better than Wendy did. He'd seen him with other girls. Alec turned on for every attractive girl he met. It didn't mean that much.

"Don't you see Alec every day at rehearsals?"

Wendy shook her head. "I've stopped going. One person can't make all the moves in a relationship. I saw Alec in the library the other day. He came right over and sat down next to me. Did you know he calls me Ranger Wendy? I think it's kind of cute, don't you?"

Was Alec being sarcastic? Marcus made no comment. Kevin, who had been asleep, was standing in the doorway staring at Wendy. Marcus picked him up. Sleep clung to the little boy's skin, and he smelled faintly of warm urine. "Say hello to Wendy."

Kevin buried his face in Marcus's shoulder. Wendy caught one of his bare feet. "Don't," Kevin said.

"Oh, Kevin, don't you like me?"

"It's awful to be so unpopular," Marcus said.

Wendy stretched out on the rug, hands under her head. Her shirt pulled out of her jeans, showing skin and the tiny knot of her belly button.

He didn't understand Alec. Wendy was a great-looking girl, and a lot of fun to be with. What did Alec want? "Move over." He and Kevin sat down on the rug next to Wendy.

That was the way they were when Karen returned, Wendy lying on the floor, and Marcus sitting next to her, talking. Kevin, still in his diapers, ran to his mother. Marcus hauled himself to his feet. "Karen, this is my friend." He motioned to Wendy. "Stand up!"

Karen nodded, and to Marcus, "I want to talk to you for a minute." He followed her into the kitchen. "Look,

I don't like surprises where Kevin is concerned. Tell me the next time you want a friend over here." It was an intense, uncomfortable moment.

Outside, Marcus wheeled his bike in silence. He was upset about Karen and wanted to blame Wendy, knew it was unfair, and kept his mouth shut.

"I don't like her so much," Wendy said, breaking the silence. "Your Karen is actually a bit of a cold fish, Marcus. Doesn't she ever smile?"

"You don't know her." He leaped to Karen's defense. "You took her by surprise. She didn't expect to see you there. She's very sensitive, very intense."

"She doesn't look healthy," Wendy said unfeelingly.

"Let's just drop the subject."

Wendy looked at him curiously. "Oh, Marcus, you've really, really got it bad, haven't you? I can't believe it!"

II

By Saturday Marcus had been working for Karen for two weeks. It was a hot spring day—people were suddenly outdoors—too beautiful a day to spend indoors with Kevin. Marcus came to work in his cutoffs, rubber clogs, and faded Baltimore Colts shirt. It was a day to be with friends, playing ball, or just drifting around, talking. "Okay with you if I take Kevin out this afternoon?" he asked Karen. "I can take him to the zoo." Karen was wearing a seersucker skirt and jacket. "You're going to be hot," she warned.

Karen, as she often did, acted as if she didn't hear what he was saying, or heard selectively. "The zoo is fine. You'll keep a close eye on Kevin? What about his nap?"

"I'll bring a blanket along. Maybe you'd like to come too?" he said boldly.

She shrugged. "Kevin," she called, "Mommy is going."

"Take the day off." He was standing close to her, his eyes fixed on the gold chain at her throat. It would be so simple to put his arms around her waist . . .

After Karen was gone he called Wendy and invited her. "Sure," Wendy said. "Meet you at the zoo."

Marcus and Kevin took the bus to the zoo and waited at the bus stop for Wendy. She came wearing a polka dot halter and denim shorts, and carrying a straw basket. "Wendy," Kevin said. "Hi, Wendy."

"See, he remembers you." Marcus patted Kevin on the head.

"Why shouldn't he remember me? I remember him. Hi, Kev, I like your outfit." He was wearing blue gym shorts, blue knee socks, and blue sneakers. "You too," she said to Marcus. "Sexy legs."

"Hairy legs turn you on?" He bumped into her. "What have you got in that interesting-looking straw basket?"

"Cookies and fruit for later."

Marcus reached around her for a cookie. She pushed him away. "I said later, grabby. Why don't you ask sometimes?"

"Ask what? I'm not a grabber. You grab plenty of times yourself." He'd been dreaming about grabbing Karen. Wendy too. That was his fantasy, to grab and to hold.

In the animal house Wendy and Kevin went from one cage to another, but Marcus remained in front of the spider monkey cage. Wendy and Kevin came back. "It's stinky here," Kevin said.

"I've had it too," Wendy said. "You ready, Marcus?"

"Not yet," he said. "See those two little guys over there, the way they're picking stuff off each other."

"Yuck! That's what's making me sick," Wendy said. "Come on, Kev, let's leave Rosenbloom to the monkeys."

Later he found them on the lawn under a tree. Wendy was swinging Kevin by his arms. "More!" Kevin shrieked. "More! Marcus, you do it."

Marcus swung Kevin in the air. "Now it's Wendy's turn." He grabbed her around the waist.

"You're looking for trouble, grabby!"

"You're looking for trouble, grabby!" Kevin echoed.

"Come on, up you go!" Marcus tried to pick her up but she made herself heavy and poked her elbows in his stomach. They were so close, he could smell the sun in her hair. "Okay, let's be friends," he said.

She slapped his hands away. "Who could be friends with a snake like you?"

"Ah, come on, Wendy," he coaxed, and got his arms around her again. He was one of those lusty men who had enough for lots of women—everything they wanted.

Wendy broke free. "Who's hungry?"

"I want a banana," Kevin said.

She handed him a banana and Marcus a carrot.

"Where's the gooey stuff?"

"This is better for you, pervert."

For Kevin's benefit, Marcus chewed the carrot like a cigar. Then they sat on the grass and watched the people going by. "Did I tell you what I decided about Alec?" Wendy said.

"No," Marcus said uncomfortably. He'd finally talked

to Alec about Wendy, and Alec had made it clear he liked Wendy, but nothing more.

"Well." Wendy straightened up. "I've decided it doesn't make any difference what I feel. I can't make something happen that isn't there. So I'm hooked, that doesn't mean I have to let myself be miserable. I'm giving up Alec! Can you give up *something* you haven't had?"

He rubbed her shoulders sympathetically.

"Oh, it's stupid!" she said. "The whole thing is stupid. I don't know how I let myself get into these things. You want to play cards?" She brought out a deck from the straw basket, then dealt them out in twos and threes.

"You could be dealing from the bottom of the deck, and I wouldn't know it." Marcus looked around for Kevin, who was pulling a fallen branch behind the tree.

Wendy studied her cards, arranged them, then snapped them shut. "Come on, play cards."

Marcus put down a jack of diamonds. Wendy picked it up, and put down a seven of clubs. No good to Marcus. He took a card from the deck. Another jack. He threw down an eight of hearts. She picked it up.

"You going to pick up every card I throw down?"

"I'm taking you for all you've got, sonny."

She felt better. He was relieved. Then Kevin walked across the cards. "No, Kevin!" Too late.

They had to start the game again. Kevin squatted down and watched Wendy deal the cards. Marcus rubbed his head. "That's a good boy, honey, you sit next to me." He studied his cards. "So who said a man and a woman can't be friends without sex?"

"I don't know, who said it?" Wendy picked up a card.

"And who is this man and woman? Not Adam and Eve."

"You and me." Marcus picked up a queen of spades Wendy had discarded. "The reason you and I don't get involved is because you're not my type."

"You mean you're not *my* type," Wendy said.

Marcus put down a king of hearts. "I'm hurt."

"I bet." She picked up the king and threw down a nine of hearts.

"I know your type." He was about to describe Alec, but felt it would be hitting too close to home. "You like jocks in high-heeled cowboy boots, with muscles in their sleeves and Bull Durhams in their mouths."

"Oh, right, and your type are sexy blondes who fall over their boobies. No other requirements necessary. Now me, I require more of a man besides basic equipment. To begin with, he's got to have brains, charm, a sense of humor—"

"I qualify on all counts," Marcus said with a modest bow.

"I like my men short, stringbean. And mysterious."

"I know, I'm an open book."

"And athletic."

"Writers sit a lot."

"You're totally unsuitable." Wendy put down her hand, three kings and a straight in clubs. "Rummy, dummy. Besides, you're a pushover at cards. You owe me sixteen cents. Pay up."

Marcus reached into his pocket. "Where's Kevin?" he said, looking around. "He was right here a moment ago."

Wendy got to her feet. "Kevin," she called.

He was nowhere on the field. "You go that way." Marcus

pointed toward the seal pond. "I'll check the animal house." He ran, expecting to see Kevin—how far could he have gone?

"Slow down," the guard in the animal house called.

"Did you see a little boy?"

"I see lotsa little boys."

Marcus ran out of the animal house. He'd been sitting around playing cards when he should have been watching Kevin. What if he didn't find him? . . . Kevin, where are you? He imagined him in the path of a car . . . or kidnapped . . . In the distance he saw Wendy waving her arm. She had Kevin by the hand. "He was chasing a squirrel."

Marcus hugged Kevin. "You got me worried." They walked back toward the bus stop. "Wendy, what if I'd really lost him? Do you realize the responsibility I have watching this kid?" He held his shirt away from his body. He was burning with relief. "You saved my life!"

"Marco, you goof. He wasn't even lost."

12

"Is it that time already?"

When Marcus arrived at Karen's she was on her knees, scraping a green chair.

"That's a nice chair. Is it oak?"

She stood up and brushed her pants. "Yes. I found it in the garage. I'm going to strip it down, if I find the time."

"I'll scrape it for you," he offered.

"I don't have the money to pay you."

"I don't care about money."

"No? You're working for money, aren't you?"

"Yes." But didn't she know it was more than money? Couldn't she tell?

"Anyway, I'd rather you spent your time with Kevin," she said. "But I appreciate your offering. Things have worked out better than I expected. Kevin really looks forward to you coming."

"I like Kevin too. I like coming here." He wanted to say more, to say everything. "I like this—" He gestured around. "This place, the pictures, everything. I like you." Oh, god, *I like you* . . . kid stuff . . . baby talk.

"I like you too, Marcus." She wiped her hands with a damp rag. "Is there any chance you can work for me tomorrow night? I know it's awfully short notice."

"No problem." But then he remembered Alec's play. He and Wendy had planned to go opening night. They could go the next night.

"You have to be a mother's dream baby-sitter. Every mother should have a Marcus." She tapped him on the shoulder. "You're really very sweet."

Later, while Kevin napped, Marcus sat with his notebook open. Karen had never asked him to baby-sit at night before. She could have gotten someone else, but she wanted him. And that thought was so full of possibilities he just sat and dreamed until the phone pulled him out of his reverie.

"Allo?" He heard a foreign voice with a heavy Russian accent. "I am looking for Marco Markovich."

"Alexandrovitch, how did you know I was here?"

"Wendy told me. I didn't know you were working. I thought you were cranking out stories in the afternoons."

"I had too much time on my hands."

"You didn't tell me."

"I didn't want to hear your wise-ass remarks about baby-sitting."

"Pretty cool, Rosenbloom. Young attractive mother in need. Marcus Rosenbloom to the rescue. Cozy setup."

"Not the kind of setup you have in mind."

"Don't disappoint me, Markovitch. You mean you're really baby-sitting? You don't have to tell me, but let me dream. Wendy said your employer could be a movie star."

"I'm just the humble baby-sitter."

"Now, maybe, but you're not stupid, you can learn. Be glad to give you a few pointers. What I called about— are you coming to the play tomorrow night? First night, everybody will be there except Pfeff, the traitor. He's on an anti-nuke action all weekend."

"Wendy and I are coming Sunday."

"Sunday night! I thought you were coming Saturday?"

"Can't. Listen, this gives you a chance to learn your lines."

"You sarcastic ass," Alec said amiably. "Sunday night's the cast party. You and Wendy want to come?"

"We'll talk about it."

"Do that. Well, it's been great talking to you."

"Yeah, it's been real exciting." A few more insults and they hung up.

Marcus took care of Kevin Saturday afternoon, then ate supper with Karen. "Nothing fancy," Karen said. "Tomato soup and toasted cheese sandwiches."

It could have been toasted straw, Marcus wouldn't have cared.

"So you're a senior," Karen said. "What happens after graduation? College?"

"I don't know. I've done some writing. I've got a story at *Playboy* magazine."

"Really? *Playboy* must pay better than I do!"

"They haven't taken it," he said lamely, explaining he was still waiting for a response. "I'll probably be turned down."

"The competition must be fierce. Every writer must want to break into *Playboy*, but all the same, you have to believe in yourself. What's the story about?"

This was just the way he'd imagined she would react, interested and encouraging. "It's about a character I made up." He told her a little about Victor Gorman.

"It sounds good." She reached over and wiped Kevin's mouth. "I like these stories about weird characters. Is it someone you know? Or is it you?"

"Me?" Marcus was genuinely surprised. "Am I weird?"

"Oh, I'm just teasing. Does your girl friend help you with your writing?"

"You mean Wendy? She's not my girl friend. We're just friends."

"You mean friend-friends?"

He nodded. "We've known each other for years."

"That is nice. When I was in school, girls and boys weren't friends, not that way. I always wanted a boy to be my friend."

He asked her where she'd studied. "Where did you learn about art? Is this your first museum job?"

"I have a Fine Arts degree from Temple." This was her first curator's job. "I haven't worked since Kevin was born, but after his father and I broke up I had to."

"Does Kevin miss his father?"

"I'm sure. Divorce is always tough on a kid. A boy needs a role model."

93

"I never knew my father while I was growing up."

"Really?" She looked at him with interest.

"It was just my mother and me. And Bill, my mother's friend."

"Well, I should be encouraged. You seem to be solidly male."

Later, while Karen got ready to go out, Marcus bathed Kevin in the tub, conscious of Karen in the other room. He lifted Kevin to the toilet seat and wrapped the towel around him.

Things had gone really well—supper together and the talk. She'd asked him questions about himself. She'd been really interested. All his impossible thoughts started to surface. Karen . . . her robe loose. . . . Damn, he was always making her robe fall open. But what had she said? *You seem to be solidly male.* That was real. He hadn't made that up.

"You won't forget to put Kevin to bed on time?" She stood at the door, dressed to go out in a long dark skirt, boots, and a corduroy jacket. Her hair was up, silver at her ears.

He dreamed of her neck, his lips in her hair . . . *Stay, don't go, stay here with me . . .*

"Wing-ding," Kevin sang. "Wingadingding-dong"

"What's that, honey? Kiss Mommy." And she was off.

After Kevin was in bed Marcus paced the apartment. *Karen . . . her head suspended like a thin piece of crystal.* . . . Should he write it down? He couldn't decide if it was inspired or idiotic. Each time he reached the front windows he looked out to see if she was coming yet. When she returned he'd help her off with her jacket. His arms would be around her, she'd lean back . . . He wouldn't

94

have to speak. She'd see everything on his face. What could they possibly say? *Karen . . . Marcus . . . Karen . . .* Great conversation.

In *The Web and the Rock,* a book he loved but nobody read any more (he'd read it six times), George Webber was a writer (like Marcus), alone and unrecognized (like Marcus). A beautiful society woman (Karen?) invites George to her house. George has just come to the city, his mind exploding with images, characters, stories. The beautiful society woman is older than George, but that doesn't matter. She loves good books and tall young writers. The walls of her living room are lined with books, the draperies are drawn, the lights low, a fire burns in the fireplace. They talk about books, art, and literature. George Webber is passionate, outspoken in his opinions.

Marcus flung out his arms. He was George Webber. And there was Karen on the couch, looking up at him. He knelt beside her. (Marcus knelt by the empty couch.) Her lips parted. She caught him in her arms, drew him down. They kissed. (Marcus embraced the pillow.) *Oh, my darling,* she said, *make love to me.* (He kissed the pillow passionately.) *Make love to me. Now!* (He lay the pillow down gently.) Rosenbloom, you incredible lover.

Later he heard Karen on the stairs. "Hello, Marcus, how's everything?" She walked in with a short, redheaded man. "How's Kevin?" Marcus looked at the man in dismay. All evening he'd been waiting for Karen to return. Marcus alone with Karen. *I'm older than you, but that doesn't matter. I love young passionate writers.*

"Marcus, this is Sid Bauer, the artist." She said "artist" as if every letter were capitalized.

"Mmmm, hmmm, mmmm, glad-a-meet-ya." The artist

stood in the middle of the room, poking out his little round belly. "Well, this is some place, Karen. I see your hand everywhere." There were paint flecks on his boots. Phony cowboy boots, phony cowboy shirt.

"What do I owe you, Marcus?" Karen said.

"I don't know."

"Let's see, you started at twelve." She counted out bills. "It's late. Sid will drive you home, won't you, Sid?"

Sid turned from examining Karen's wall hangings. "Of course, if you promise me a cup of coffee afterward, and something sweet."

"I don't need a ride." Marcus spoke in a muffled voice.

"You sure?" the artist said indifferently.

Marcus didn't look at him but snatched the money Karen was holding out, and rushed from the apartment.

13

"This came in yesterday's mail," Sally said, handing him a manila envelope. She was in her robe. It was Sunday morning. The envelope was creased in the middle, and Marcus saw at once that it was the same self-addressed envelope he'd sent *Playboy* with his story. Did it have an acceptance? Or was his story inside, rejected, come back to him? He went weak with fear and couldn't open it. *Oh, god*, he prayed, *let it be something good.*

Dear Mr. Rosenbloom. Dear Mr. Genius. Dear Incredible New Writing Discovery. And there would be a check. *Usually we pay $500, but since your story was so outstanding we enclose a check for $5000.*

In his room he threw the envelope on the bed. Too fat to be just a letter and a check. The manuscript was inside. Open it! In the mirror he looked himself bravely in the face. Open the envelope. If you're going to be killed, face it.

He tore open the flap. There was a brief printed note attached to his manuscript. "Thank you for submitting your manuscript to us, but at this time . . ." Blah, blah blah. He crumpled the note, then kicked it under the bed.

That night Marcus had his mother's car. He wore a fawn-colored turtleneck and his old tweed jacket. He had pushed the rejection of his story out of his mind. Well, not completely, but he wasn't going to think about it or talk about it either.

Wendy sneezed when she met him at the door of her aunt's house. She wore a skirt and heels and carried a leather pocketbook. "It's my aunt's and it's full of tissues," she said hoarsely. She sneezed again. "I woke up with this cold this morning." Her nose was red. "Let me say good-bye to my aunt and uncle."

Aunt Ginny and Uncle Doug were in the living room playing backgammon. "Hello, Marcus," Aunt Ginny said. "You look nice."

Uncle Doug, still in the white coveralls of the laundry company he drove for, gave Marcus an unenthusiastic look. "You go to that play tonight, Wen, and you're *really* going to get sick."

"I have to go, Uncle Doug." She sneezed again, then kissed her aunt and uncle. "Don't you guys wait up for me."

In the car she kept the tissues in her lap. "How do I look, Marcus?"

"You want the truth, or a nice lie?"

"Forget it." She reached for a fresh tissue and blew, then for another one to wipe her dripping eyes.

"Maybe you should stay home?"

"No. Alec called to see if I was coming, and I promised. What will he think if I don't show up?"

"Probably won't notice the difference."

"Thanks a lot. You are a grump."

He grunted.

Wendy reached for a tissue. "Well, how's the fair Karen?"

"No comment."

"Okay, how's the writing going?"

"I don't want to talk about that either."

Wendy sniffled. "Nice day, isn't it?"

Marcus maintained a rude silence, remembering the rejection of his story. Every time he thought of it, it made him feel sick. "*Playboy* rejected my story," he said at last.

"What? My ears are plugged."

"*Playboy* rejected my story," he said loudly. He'd be yelling in a minute. "They returned it, untouched, unread. They didn't want it."

"I'm sorry." Wendy touched his arm. "I know how much it meant to you."

"Forget it."

"Fine, I will!" She drew away. Now they were both sitting in stubborn silence.

Marcus felt he'd acted like a fool, and when they reached the theater he said, "Wendy, I apologize." He put his hand to his heart. "Humbly and sincerely. I've acted like a crumb tonight."

"Did you say crud?"

"I'm not the easiest person to be around sometimes."

"No comment."

"You have to admit I'm making a sincere effort to change."

"I've hardly noticed."

"Do you have to disagree with everything I say?"

"Why should I agree with you when you're always wrong?"

They parked and walked toward the theater. Wendy wobbled on her heels, and clutched Marcus's arm. "Isn't that the ultimate? Wear heels and you've got to hang on to a man." She bumped into him and he bumped her back in a friendly way.

All through the first act of the play, Wendy muffled her sneezes, but during the second act she started sneezing so violently she had to run out. Marcus joined her during intermission. "Maybe I should drive you home, Wen. You really look beat."

"No, I'm staying."

She felt better through the third act, and they stood for the curtain calls, both of them saving their loudest applause for Alec. "I kept wishing," Wendy said, "he'd make a mistake, so I could laugh at him, but he was wonderful."

"He was good."

"He was the outstanding actor, Marcus, and you know it."

It was true. Then why was he feeling so negative? Because all through the play he kept remembering his story, and how Karen had come back with that fat little artist last night.

Backstage, Alec, still in costume, was hyped up, embracing and kissing everyone. The makeup made him look as if he were still acting. Terri came over and he gave her a long passionate kiss on the mouth. Then he noticed them and put his arms out. "Marc! Wendy!" He embraced Marcus, then caught Wendy around the waist and kissed her on the mouth.

"You were wonderful," she said. She was flushed and her eyes shone with excitement. She didn't look the least bit sick any more.

A woman threw her arms around Alec's neck. "Sweets, you were wonderful." A moment later Terri caught his hand and they went off somewhere.

Marcus and Wendy stood on the side waiting for Alec to return. "How long do you think we should wait?" Wendy said.

"I'm ready to go right now."

"Let's give them a few more minutes." She pulled Marcus out of the way of a ladder coming through.

They stood around a little longer. "I don't know what we're doing here," Wendy finally said. "Let's go."

Outside they walked along in silence. Wendy removed her heels and walked in her stockinged feet. "Did you notice Alec just came up to my shoulder?" She gave a long sigh.

"I thought you were off Alec," Marcus said.

"I'm trying to be."

Marcus knew what that meant. "Me too."

"Does that mean Karen?"

"Yeah, it's crazy."

"We both are crazy," Wendy said, and put her arm around his waist.

14

Karen wore a gown decorated with tiny flowers, her hair loose. "If Kevin's father calls, will you tell him to call me tomorrow?" Marcus nodded. "Bye-bye, baby," she called to Kevin, who was playing on the floor.

After she left, Marcus stood by the window. Across the street Bauer, the artist, held the car door open for her. Why was he hanging inside the door so long? What did she see in that potbellied, redheaded, little show-off? It was miserable being in love. Better to have a broken leg. Write it down, he told himself. The last conference he'd had with Sweeny, the teacher had told him he had to keep writing. Sweeny had had a fit when he heard Marcus had thrown away the Victor Gorman piece. "Wrong. I want you to retype that story and mail it to another magazine. If you're going to be defeated by one rejection—" Sweeny went at him like a coach. "Get off your tail! I'll expect you to have pages next time on that Isabel story." He picked up his red pencil. Dismissed.

So now Marcus sat with his notebook. "Isabel," he wrote, "you'll never know what you did to me." He sat there and tried to remember how it had been in sixth grade when he'd sat behind Isabel in Miss Black's class.

Later, he was putting Kevin in his pajamas when the downstairs buzzer rang. A man in a red blazer, a box under his arm, was at the door.

"I'm Bob Lambert." He looked at Marcus curiously. "Where's Karen? I'm Kevin's father."

"Karen's out right now. I'm the babysitter. Marcus Rosenbloom."

They shook hands. There was something formal and stiff about Bob Lambert. He didn't look like he belonged with Karen. He looked like a minister or a principal.

Lambert ran upstairs and lifted his son into his arms. Kevin pushed his father's hat back and pinched his nose.

"Don't you want to kiss your daddy? Do you want to see the nice present I brought you?"

"Are you my same daddy? Put me down."

"The very same." Lambert opened the package and held out a large, gray teddy bear. "You can sleep with Teddy tonight."

Kevin took the animal. "What else?" he said.

Watching them, Marcus felt something familiar about the scene, an echo of his own childhood. A father returning to his son. Not that his own father had ever been like this. No, this was the old dream of the way his father would return to him someday.

It was past one o'clock when Marcus heard Karen's steps on the stairs. "Marcus?" She was alone. "I thought you'd be asleep. How'd everything go?"

"Fine." He searched her face. As always, her eyes were elsewhere. "Kevin's father came to see him."

"And you let him in?"

"Yes," he said, surprised at her anger.

"Who gave you permission? He's got no business here, do you understand? Not when I'm not here. And he knows it. You're never to let him in without my permission."

"Okay," he said. "I get it." She didn't have to pound him over the head. He felt wrongly accused, didn't want her talking to him like that. "It won't happen next time."

"Where's Kevin?"

"Sleeping. Karen, it's all right. He brought Kevin a teddy bear."

She brushed past him. "I bet he did!" He followed her into Kevin's room. She leaned over Kevin, straightening his blanket, then picked up the teddy bear. They stood in the dimly lit hall. "Is this what he brought?"

"He was only here for a few minutes," Marcus whispered.

"He isn't going to have things his own way. Comes when he damn pleases, thinks he can still bully me around. Well, he can't."

"Look, I'm sorry. I really didn't know."

She slumped against the wall and started rubbing her temples nervously. "I just hate the constant fighting."

In the narrow hall his hand was on the wall near her face. So close. He felt she wanted something from him. "I'll never let him in again." Ordinary words. "You can count on me." Words couldn't convey what he felt. More than words . . . he wanted. . . . His hands fell to her arms. He pulled her toward him, leaned toward her, tried to kiss her.

She pushed him away.

"Please . . . I mean . . . Let me . . ."

"For god's sake, Marcus!" She got away from him. "What do you think you're doing? You catch me when I'm upset— Because I'm alone, you think— Oh, no! Oh, no! I can manage very well, thank you. I don't need your kind of help."

"I didn't—" He tried to speak, to explain. "I didn't mean—"

"Oh, you did! You *did* mean. Don't tell me you didn't! Aah, men! And I suppose you think I should be grateful. No, thank you." She pushed him down the hall, hitting him with the teddy bear. "All right, go, go home now. Just go! And don't bother coming back."

Marcus rode through the dark, deserted streets, head down, wobbling on his bike from one side of the street to the other. He rode through the light cast by street lamps, then darkness, then light, then darkness. He choked up, groaned, hit himself. He'd begged her. How could he have begged? *Please, let me.* "Oh, oh, oh."

Wendy's house was dark. He rapped on her window. "Wendy, it's me, Marcus."

The shade came up, and her face appeared. "Marcus?"

"I have to talk to you. Open up."

She opened the door, wrapped in a blanket. "What happened? It's after two o'clock." He followed her into the dark room. "Don't turn on the light," she said, "and keep your voice down or you'll wake them. Wait a minute, I want to wash my face." She went out.

Marcus scrunched down in the chair. It was close inside, a close night smell, hair, something musky. . . . His eyes burned. Wendy returned, climbed into bed, and pulled the covers around her shoulders. "You cold? You want a blanket?"

Marcus sank deeper into the chair, shutting his eyes. For a minute he couldn't speak. Then he told her. "I blew it, Wendy. I made a pass at Karen. How could I have done it? How could I have been so stupid?"

"It isn't stupid to want someone, to love them, Marcus."

"You don't understand! She didn't want me." He went to the window, looked out, then sat on the bed next to Wendy. "She hates me, despises me. I can't go back there." Tears squeezed from his eyes. Wendy put her arms around him. He let himself be held, aware of the scratchy blanket against his cheek, aware of the rise and fall of her breast. He was in pain. He was aware of his pain. He hurt. I hurt, he thought. This is pain, this is grief, this is what loving someone and not being loved in return feels like. He hurt, and in a part of his mind he gloried in his hurt. Now he knew pain, he could weep, he was experiencing something real and awful. And through all that he was also conscious of Wendy's holding him against her breast, her hand on his head.

I5

In the bathroom, Marcus, a towel around his waist, brushed his teeth. Yesterday, all day, he'd waited for a message from Karen, a summons to return. *All is forgiven.* Why had she gotten so angry? Because he needed her, wanted her? Was that so wrong? Was that potbellied artist better than him?

He stuck out his tongue—ugh!—and brushed that. In the other room Wendy was talking to Sally. Wendy was here—good. Maybe he'd streak through the living room, and cheer everyone up.

Pants on, shirt tucked in. Grab some bills from the bureau. He was ready to fly. "Wendy, you coming?"

"What's your rush?" Sally said. "I haven't seen you all week."

"No time for small talk. Gotta fly, Sally. Wendy, let's go." And he was out of the apartment.

"How do you feel, Marcus?"

He put his finger to his head and pulled the trigger.

"That bad?" Wendy's hair stood out around her head like a halo.

Marcus crossed the highway to the Donut Shoppe. Forget Karen . . . forget her. . . . How could he have begged her? He'd pretended his feelings were so pure and elevated. Love and adoration. But all the time the beast in him had wanted to put his hands on her breasts. Marcus the Beast. That's what he was. He could feel the skin tighten around his mouth, his lips twist cynically. The lips of cynicism, burned into his face forever. Cold, disdainful lips, a face that made women tremble. He checked his sneer in the window of the Donut Shoppe. A little too theatrical.

Inside, a cute girl in a pink uniform waited on them. She had a fat little mouth, a fat, hot, greasy little mouth. He ordered a headlight, a taillight, a cinnamon, a Dutch apple, a chocolate-covered donut, and two Bavarian cremes. "What'll you have, Wendy?"

"Indigestion."

He took the donuts in a white bag, and then they jogged toward the park, where he threw himself down on the grass and looked up at the sky. "Wendy B., you are patient, kind, and good to put up with me."

"You're telling me." She broke apart a Bavarian creme and gave him half.

"You know what I'd like to do with this donut?" Marcus said. "Push it into Karen's face."

"You act like she did something to you."

"She did. She made me want her. She made me want to kiss her."

"That isn't what you told me before."

"Wendy, whose side are you on?"

"Is this a war? You grabbed her. She didn't grab you. You attacked her."

"Attacked!" Marcus sat up. "So now I'm a criminal." He threw the donut down. "Jesus, Wendy, I kissed her, that's all. Is that a crime? In the total order of crimes, from swiping a kid's lollipop to murder, where does stealing a kiss fit? Where would you put it, Wendy? Is it high crime or low? If you want to know what I think, I did her a favor kissing her."

"If you want to know what I think, you took what you had no right to take."

He looked off. Past the trees, some men were playing baseball. "You sang a different tune the other night."

"You were in pain then."

"I'm still in pain. Am I that awful? I brush my teeth every day. Do I smell, Wendy? You'd tell me if I did, wouldn't you? What makes her so perfect, so much better than me that she can abuse me?"

"Abuse you? I don't believe this."

"She hit me with the teddy bear. Don't laugh. Nobody likes to be hit with a teddy bear. What if I kissed you? Would you hit me with a teddy bear?" He reached over and pulled her toward him.

"Marcus!" She raised a donut.

"Do it." He thrust his face forward. "Right into my mouth, mash me."

"Don't tempt me."

"Come on, just mash me. I've always wanted to be hit with a jelly donut."

"I can just hear you crying to the police: 'That woman just assaulted me with a jelly donut.' They'll file it with your other report of assault and battery with a teddy bear."

Marcus fell back on the ground, put his hands behind his head. "I don't want to talk about Karen anymore. I'm sick of the subject. You're right, Wendy, I shouldn't have touched her. I know it, but I still hate her."

"You ought to stop thinking about her."

"Aren't you still thinking about Alec?"

She shrugged.

"See. You're still thinking about him."

"No, I'm not! Not much, anyways."

Marcus ruffled her hair. "You can always cry on my manly shoulders, Wendy. I've been crying on yours enough."

Tuesday, Bill came home, looking brown and fit, and there was a lot of excitement. Bill grasped Marcus's hand, gripped his shoulder. A muscular male greeting. It was good to have Bill back.

Sally brought out the liquor bottles from the bottom of the cupboard and put them on a serving cart in the dining room. She never drank when Bill was away. Bill poured wine for each of them.

"Oh, before I forget," Sally said, putting down her glass. "There was a phone call for you, Marcus. The woman you work for wants you to stop by."

Marcus sat down, worked the drink around in his hand, then put it down. "I'm going out," he said. "There's something I have to do." He hooked his bike over his shoulder and hurried out.

At Karen's house he rang the bell, then stood back. Don't act too eager, he told himself, but he was sweating. He heard steps on the stairs. Then the door opened a crack and a girl squinted at him suspiciously. "What do you want?"

"Where's Karen?"

"Out. Who are you? Are you Marcus?"

"Yes."

"Wait, I've got something for you." She ran back upstairs and returned. "Here." She handed him a white envelope. "She said to give this to you, if you came."

He folded the envelope in half and put it into his breast pocket. "Did she say anything else . . . about coming back?"

"No."

He nodded and turned away. When he was around the corner he opened the envelope. There was money inside, the exact amount she owed him for baby-sitting. Not a word, not even his name on the outside. He pocketed the money and threw away the envelope.

16

(From Marcus's notebook)

Walking Down Wyoming Street

Past houses and bushes and under trees,
Where roots push the sidewalk up,
Through sunshine and shade we're moving,
And you're talking, and I'm listening,
Or I'm talking and you're listening.
You notice the plants some lady has up on her
     porch in tomato-juice cans,
And I point to the sky-blue color somebody has painted
     their house.
And I get that friendship feeling,
That talking-and-walking-down-Wyoming-Street
With-my-friend-Wendy feeling.

17

The money Karen had paid Marcus sat on the bureau in his glass penny jar. Each time he saw the crumpled bills he remembered. It was like a closed door opening a crack. It hurt, and he pulled it shut fast.

It wasn't Karen, anymore. He could forget Karen. He *was* forgetting her. But the memory of what an ass he'd made of himself lingered. It was something he was never, never, *never* going to do again—if he could help it—which he doubted.

These days he felt close to Wendy because they'd been through something together. Well, not exactly together, but she'd helped him, and the things they'd felt and the disappointments they'd both had gave them a lot in common.

He was sick of looking at Karen's money, and decided to have a party with it. He asked Wendy if she wanted to help him celebrate. "This is going to be a how-I-kicked-the-habit party. It's on Karen."

"We'll make it a double celebration," Wendy said. "I talked to Alec today. I was right up next to him, and I hardly got a twinge."

They went to the Persian Room. Marcus wore blue slacks and a white jacket he'd borrowed from Bill, and Wendy looked really different with her hair pulled back, and wearing a green velvet dress with thin straps that showed her shoulders.

When the waiter brought the menu and Marcus saw the prices, they had a quick conference on what they could order. No lobster tonight, and they had to leave a fair tip. No dessert either. Marcus wanted Wendy to order first so she could have something good. "Why don't you order the shrimp? I'll have the French leek soup."

"I should have brought some money with me," Wendy said.

"It's my party," he said. "Go ahead, order. I've always wanted to try French leek soup."

When their orders came there was only a small cup of soup, but he made it last by eating it slowly. "It's *nothing*," Wendy whispered. "Did you see what they charged for that?"

"It's the best leek soup I've ever had."

"It's the only leek soup you've ever had. Here, take some of mine."

Marcus looked around. He didn't see anyone else sharing their food. "We better not."

"I'm not going to eat and have you starving," Wendy said. She pushed her plate toward him.

He thought people were looking at them, thinking they were a couple, at least going together. Being here, dressed up, he felt different, as if they really were a couple. He liked the way Wendy was sitting, and the careful way she ate. Neither of them was completely at ease, but still, as Wendy whispered to him, he felt they were as good as any of these elegant couples around them.

He kept glancing at Wendy. What if they were really going together? Neither of them had anybody and they liked each other. He'd never noticed before what really nice hands she had. And her shoulders, and the way her ears lay against her head. It was funny, because he'd never thought about her shoulders or ears before, or her legs either. They kept bumping into each other under the table. "Oops," Wendy said and drew her legs back. He did too, but he wanted to bump knees again, maybe catch her legs between his.

Jesus! King George was awake. Just the thought of Wendy's legs. . . .

Marcus shifted uncomfortably. "What's the matter Marcus?"

"I've got a charley horse in my leg."

"Stand on it," she advised. "That's the only way to get rid of it."

"No, that's all right."

"Do it. Don't be embarrassed. If you're in pain—Nobody's going to say anything."

He forced a smile. "It's okay now." But every time he looked at Wendy he was in trouble again. He just couldn't control it. He thought how frustrated they'd both been over other people. What if they were going together, wouldn't that solve all their problems?

And then he realized he was thinking like a pig, thinking only about himself. It was the sex thing, that horniness in him that fastened on to any female he was near. He still hadn't forgotten the time he'd fallen on Wendy and what she'd said. She'd made it clear that they were just friends. Still he couldn't keep from thinking how perfect it would be, neither of them with anybody special of their own, both of them stuck on the kiddie side of the wall. He was ready to say something, but he didn't want it to come out wrong.

"Look, Karen—"

"*Karen?*"

He stopped, horrified, and struck himself in the head. "Wendy, Wendy, Wendy!"

Wendy got a little red.

"Wendy, I wasn't thinking about her. I was thinking about *you,* about us, about the way we are together." He had her attention now. "What I'm thinking . . ." He worked the glass of water around and around. "I think I have a solution to our problem."

"I didn't know we had one."

"You know, you with Alec, and me with Karen." Then his nerve failed him and he said, "We'll probably be doing things together this summer, right? So why don't we go together officially?"

"Go together?" she repeated.

"You know: boy-girl. You Jane, me Tarzan."

"We are together," Wendy said.

"Just friends, though." He got embarrassed then, because this other idea was in his head and he wasn't expressing it. "If we go together, then we belong together." He put his fingers over his eyes. "I can't talk about this. Do I sound like an idiot?" He was reverting. The Complete Adolescent. He pulled himself up. "Okay, Wendy, forget what I just said. Let's start again. Remember that time we were in the mall and then we walked to your aunt's and talked about experience? I told you I didn't have any, and you were surprised, and then you said the same thing."

She nodded. "I remember."

"Does that still hold?"

"Do you mean, did something happen with Alec? I told you, nothing happened, Marcus."

"I thought so, but I want to be sure."

"What's the matter?" Wendy said. "You won't associate with a girl who's done it?"

"No, no!" She was getting it all wrong. "Look, we're friends. I like you; we like each other. We'd be, well, helping each other out." If she didn't get that part, she was hopeless.

"What would we do that was different from now?" Wendy said.

She didn't get it. "I wish you weren't so dense," he said. "What do people do when they go together, Wendy?"

"Oh, Oh! You mean boyfriend and girlfriend."

"You make it sound like Beauty and the Beast. Come on, Wendy, it's hard enough talking about it without you being dumb about it."

117

"Okay, I get it. You want us to go together."

"Right, right."

"Oh," she said. "Oh, I never thought that you and I—"

"Right," he said. "Have I told you my wall theory?"

"What wall is that?"

"It's like the Great Wall of China, only this wall is bigger and longer and goes all around the world. It divides the whole human race. Every human being is either on one side of the wall or the other."

"I hope we're on the same side, Marcus."

"We are, but it's the wrong side. We're on the side with the babies."

"That's nice."

"Only if you're a baby. When you grow up you realize it's the wrong side of the wall and you want to get over on the other side with the big people. Everyone wants to get over that wall but they can't do it by themselves. Two people have to go over the wall together. Sometimes two people on the wrong side help each other." Marcus paused. "If they're friends and like each other."

"Like you and me?"

"Exactly! Well, what do you say, Wendy?"

"About what?"

"The *wall*," Marcus said. She could be so thick sometimes.

"I know about that wall," Wendy said.

"Well?"

"Well, what?"

Every time she said "what" she made him feel like a fool. "Do you want to go over that wall with me or not?"

"I've thought about it."

She really got to him, the way she said it, so calmly.

"Sure, I've thought about it. A lot of times I feel I just want to climb over and not kill myself, and be on the other side."

"But not with me?"

"I wouldn't say that. I've thought about a lot of possibilities."

"What did you think about me?"

"For a long time I thought we'd always be just friends. Even that time when you made me so mad coming down on top of me like a big ox. Afterward, I felt sorry, you were so embarrassed. I really loved you then. I've always loved you, but, you know, like a friend."

"And friends don't?"

"No, maybe friends do. Maybe that's the best way of all. I've been waiting for lightning to strike, but that can scare you too, like with Alec."

Why was she bringing Alec up now? Because she still liked him, that's why, liked Alec a lot more than she liked Marcus.

"I think I got so excited about Alec because I was feeling so alone. New school, by myself so much. I thought he was so sensitive at first."

"Alec? Sensitive?" Oh, this really hurt.

"I know Alec didn't feel about me the way I felt about him."

"You bet he didn't!"

"For a while I thought Alec was interested, really cared. I know I could have let myself go with him."

"You already said that."

Wendy looked at him. "This is upsetting you. I thought we could be open with each other."

Yes, yes, he agreed. He put on his serious, I'm-listening-to-you-Wendy expression. Dr. Fraud looking intelligent.

"What if Karen called you back now? What if she said, Come back, Marcus. Would you go?"

"No, not now." Said it and knew he lied. He still dreamed about Karen, but in these dreams he didn't beg. And he got what he wanted. He dreamed about Bev and about Wendy, too, and all his dreams were for him, his need, his satisfaction. It was selfish, he was selfish, that was the truth. How was he supposed to explain that to Wendy?

"Alec and I were never friends, not the way *we* are, Marcus. I guess that's why this really makes sense to me. I mean, climbing that wall together."

"It does! You do!"

"Yes, but we can't take chances."

"I understand. Do you want to take care of it? Can you get the pill?"

"I don't want to. It had a bad effect on my mother."

"What does she use, then?"

"The coil, but that's no good if you've never had sex."

"Oh, then it's up to me. I'll take care of it."

"Maybe somebody else would think this is, you know, a little cold-blooded. I never thought I'd be talking this way myself. But we are talking, and I'm glad. I guess we're making an agreement."

"We are, we certainly are."

"It feels right." Wendy spoke softly. "There's no other boy I like as much as I like you, Marcus. I feel good about you, and we trust each other, and we're friends."

"Wendy," he said taking her hand. "This is going to make us better friends than ever."

18

**BARRETT AND ROSENBLOOM IN AGREEMENT
ON DELICATE SUBJECT. DETAILS
STILL UNDISCLOSED.**

After a period of round-the-clock negotia-
tions, Marcus Rosenbloom and Wendy Barrett have reached an agreement on a delicate
subject, the agreement to be implemented in
an as-yet-undesignated location, sometime
soon. The two young people have no one else
to do it with, are tired of waiting for it to
happen, and know they can trust each other
not to be moody, ugly, exploitive, or sensa-
tional about the upcoming event.

19

Marcus wandered around the drugstore, checking first the cigarette and tobacco counter where they kept the *Playboy* magazines out of reach. Then he checked among the cosmetics, dental supplies, mouthwashes, bandages, stationery, vitamins, shampoos, combs and brushes, Pampers . . . Everything but what he wanted. Finally he went up to the prescription counter, where he picked up a jar of Noxema and a handful of ballpoint pens so it wouldn't look like he was only in there for one thing. He was a bona fide buyer.

He waited till the pharmacist was free, then stepped up to the counter. The pharmacist was above him. With his sharp beak and blue rosy jowls, he looked like a rooster. Marcus had his question all prepared, but all that came out was, "Rubbers?"

"Rubbers?" The man frowned. "Do you mean rain shoes?"

"Rubbers," Marcus repeated, his voice fading. What was the other name? "Rubbers. You know, *rubbers.*"

"Prophylactics?"

"Yes, sir."

"Why didn't you say so?" The pharmacist looked over Marcus's head. Was he signaling someone? The police: *move in and grab this pervert.*

"Any particular brand?" On the shelf behind him there were rows of neat, colorful boxes.

"Brand? No. It doesn't matter."

"What style?"

Was there more than one? Was it like buying a suit? Did he want a conservative style, Western, something flashy?

"Natural, ribbed, extra sensitive. We've got them in color too."

"Something regular," Marcus said, "average. The ordinary ones."

The pharmacist handed him a small plastic box with a picture of a girl with windblown hair that reminded him of Terri. Easy Riders.

"How many boxes?"

"How many in a box?"

"A dozen."

A dozen ought to hold him for the rest of his life. He took two boxes just because he might never get the nerve to do this again. He walked away with the boxes and his other purchases, then waited till there was nobody at the checkout counter. The girl at the register looked vaguely familiar. She put the articles into a bag, sealed the top with register tape, then handed him his change. He took his loot and fled.

20

"Hi, Marcus." Wendy met him at the door wearing dark blue corduroy pants and a pink T-shirt. "Say hello to my aunt and uncle. I told them I was going out."

Marcus poked his head into the kitchen. "Hello." Aunt Ginny and Uncle Doug were at the table, smoking and drinking coffee. "It's me," Marcus said. Enough? He was ready to go. Wendy's aunt was always friendly, but he didn't know how to take her uncle.

"How's the weather?" Ginny said.

"Warm. Nice."

"You kids going to take a walk, or what?"

"Right, a walk."

Uncle Doug looked at Marcus as if he knew exactly what was on Marcus's mind.

And what *was* on his mind? Things. *Things?* he could imagine Wendy saying, *what* things *are you speaking of?*

It, he would say. *You know, what we talked about. The wall.*

It? Things? The wall? Is there another word? Can you be more specific, Marcus?

Of course. Writers can always be more specific. We're going to park on Brick Yard Falls Road . . . climb the hill behind Techumseh School . . . cozy down on a blanket behind some big old mauseleum in St. Mary's Cemetery . . . and everywhere we go, we're—

"Better take an umbrella, Wendy," Uncle Doug said. "It's drizzling out." He didn't trust Marcus's weather reports, either.

Outside they sauntered along together. "Your aunt's a lot friendlier than your uncle."

"Uncle Doug? That's just the way he is. He's really sweet. Where are we going?"

"I don't know, just walking. Let's go over to the campus."

They bumped into each other and he put his arm around her waist. Was she thinking the way he was? She hadn't said anything, but then neither had he. Talk was so crude and inadequate. He didn't want Wendy to think he had only one vulgar subject on his mind, even if he did. Talking about sex, he recognized, embarrassed him; even thinking about talking about it embarrassed him. And when you were nearly eighteen years old, that was pathetic.

"Do you remember what we were talking about in the restaurant?" Wendy said.

He gave her a squeeze and she squeezed back. "Sure, I do."

"So are we going together? Is this our first date?"

Marcus picked up an aluminum soda tab and put it on her finger. "Now it's official."

"Oh, Marcus," Wendy fluttered, "it's so beautiful. Now what's our favorite food?"

"Freihoffer's chocolate chip cookies."

"And our own song?"

" 'Row, Row, Row Your Boat,' " Marcus said. "It's been my favorite song since kindergarten."

Wendy put her arm through his. "Let's go to K Mart sometime, and pick out matching shirts, something with big red hearts to wear to school so everybody knows. And we'll hold hands in assembly and in the halls. Do you like holding hands, Marcus?"

"Ahem." Professor Fraud cleared his throat. "Good for a while, but definitely limited. A hangover from the old days when that was all kids were allowed to do. A form of handcuff. As long as kids were holding hands, their hands weren't other places."

Yes, definitely limited. *Today there are a lot more things for kids to do than that, Wendy.*

Ahem, Miss Barrett, I wonder if you'd consider a little sport?

Sport, Mr. Rosenbloom? What game do you have in mind?

It's a new game. No, not really that new—just to us—but I hear it's great fun.

It started to rain a little harder. Before them, the massive university library was brightly lit. "Let's go in there," Marcus said. Maybe they could get into one of the carrels together and make out, or fall into each other's arms between the stacks. The building was new, and the floors carpeted. Maybe they could thrash around in an out of the way corner. They'd fit in anywhere, a typical college pair engaged in Interpersonal Relations 101 . . . or was it Small Group Interaction 453?

They went down the stairs to the newspaper and periodical room and amused themselves for a while looking at the papers from all over the world. The only other person in the room was an Indian student with slick black hair and lips the color of plums. If he left they would be all alone. Maybe they could creep under the racks and cover themselves with the *New York Times*.

"See if there are any help-wanted ads in London," Wendy directed. "Or Paris; Paris is better. I'd like to go there and work, and learn to speak real Parisian French."

For a while they deciphered the headlines in French and Italian, but were defeated by the Arabic. Marcus also gave up on the Indian student leaving. They rode the elevator upstairs and wandered through the stacks. There were people everywhere. "Let's go someplace else," he said.

They walked over to Marshall Street, stopping to buy ice cream cones. Wendy had hers dipped in hot fudge. A gentle rain fell, a soft spring drizzle. Wendy took off her sneakers and walked barefoot. Outside the Engineering Building they leaned against a stone sculpture of a mother and child and kissed. Their first real kiss. The only parts of them that touched were their lips. Hers were wet and sweet from the fudge. He pushed a little. She pushed back. Their lips pressed hard together. He wanted to pause and ask, How's that? but he didn't want to stop this good feeling ever. Why hadn't he thought to kiss Wendy sooner?

They kissed again. Her lips parted. He was having trouble catching his breath. Wendy pressed against him and they continued kissing.

21

Sunday afternoon, playing cards on Wendy's bed. Rain spattered the windows. "Let it rain," Marcus hummed studying his cards. "Let it pour. Ummm."

"Ummm what?" Wendy said. She picked up a card. "Rummy. I win."

"I lose, you win," he sang. He leaned forward and kissed Wendy on the mouth. They played another hand. He hummed, shelled peanuts, and fed them to Wendy. "Open up, Wendybird."

"Play your cards, turkey."

"Ummm." His eyes were on his cards, on Wendy, on the long green sweater she wore with the sleeves pushed up.

"Ummm." Dr. Horney says it's checkup time. . . . Yes, Doctor . . . your . . . your . . . Anything you say, Doctor . . .

"Ummm." Let it rain . . . let it rain . . . the rain song . . . The Wendy and Marcus song . . . the how-am-I-going-to-get-my-hands-around-her song. It was an inside, out-of-the-rain song, cozy and mellow. It gave him a glow in the pit of his being, because something good was going to happen soon, very soon. "Ummm."

"I like to hear you singing, Marcus."

"She'll be coming round the mountain when she comes." He tapped time on Wendy's knee. "When she comes." He'd sing her into his arms. "Sunday afternoon, in the rain with my baby. Sunday afternoon with my honey."

"Nice voice."

"You and I," he sang, putting his hand over his heart, "can make beautiful music together."

Get it, Wendy? Did she get it? He sang earnestly leaning toward her, smiling, caressing her with his smile, bedroom smile.

"Are you looking at my cards, you cheat?"

He sniffed her hair, her neck.

"Marcus, that tickles."

Didn't she get it? Couldn't she read him? *What are we waiting for Wendy, my sweet?*

Through the wall he heard the low hum of the refrigerator and the rumble of the television. *We are alone, Wendy. The door is shut. Drop your cards and let's embrace. I want to kiss your sweet, sweet face.*

"Rummy," Wendy said, showing her cards. "I can't believe how easy you are to beat."

"Let's do something else," he said. "Cards bore me."

131

"It's raining."

"We don't have to go out."

"Marcus, I don't think this is the best place."

"Why not?" he said, and reached for her so hard she fell off the bed. "Oh, Wendy!" He lay there for a moment smiling down at her.

They kissed on the floor, pressed hard together. She had her arm around his neck. He was fumbling with her buttons, and she kept turning so he couldn't get at them. She finally got to her knees and belted him with the pillow. "Pest!" Her shirt was pulled out, her hair frizzed. "Fight for your life!" He dove for her. She stood on the bed and hit him with the pillow. They scuffled. Wendy was hitting him as hard as she could. He couldn't stop grabbing.

"Hit me, Wendy, I'm going to get you."

She caught him in the face with the pillow. He got his arms around her legs and pulled her down.

"What the hell's going on in there?" Uncle Doug was outside the door. "What are you kids doing? Sounds like you're pulling the building down."

Marcus fell back into the chair.

"Sorry, Uncle Doug." Wendy tucked her shirt in. "We were just having a pillow fight. I'm giving Marcus a little lesson."

Oh, yes. Marcus lay back and looked at Wendy with happy eyes. *Teach me, Wendy. Teach me everything you know.*

"Keep it down," Uncle Doug said.

"You see what I mean?" Wendy said. She felt her hair, then combed it.

Marcus put out his arms and pulled Wendy into his lap.

"You're so grabby."

"I'll be nicer. Will you be nicer?"

"I'm too nice to you already."

They lay on the bed again and kissed and petted, and he was ready and eager, and, oh, so willing, and she was soft and warm and a little reluctant, and there was confusion on the bed and mixed-up signals, and fumbling and reaching. Just a little bit more . . . a little bit. Did she want to? . . . Did she want to? . . . She just had to. . . .

"Uncle Doug?"

"He won't come in."

Clothes, buttons, hooks, zippers. Clumsy fingers. Whispers. "Do you have something?"

"Got it." In his wallet, tucked away in a secret compartment, neatly rolled in silver, sanitized, safe.

"Wait. I think I hear them."

"Don't worry." Mr. Calm and Friendly. But underneath he was trembling, he was so eager and scared and full of wanting.

"Marcus, somebody's in the kitchen."

Fumbling, bumbling, crumbling. . . . Oh, god, he was collapsing. Oh, King George, you traitor. You Abdicator. He rolled off the bed.

"Hey, Wendy," Uncle Doug called. "I'm making toasted cheese sandwiches. You want one?"

Wendy sat up and pulled down her sweater. "No thanks, Uncle Doug." Then in a whisper to Marcus, "Good thing we stopped. He was practically in the room."

Silence.

"Look, we've just got to plan things better."

Silence.

"The place is wrong, you have to admit that. We can't just do it in this dumb way."

Silence.

"I mean, did we even know what we were doing?"

Silence.

"Marcus, will you say something. Talk!"

SILENCE.

Marcus walked home in the rain, shucked off his wet clothes, and sat on the kitchen counter, lotus fashion, with a cup of hot milk. Sally and Bill were out. He heard the clock in the living room ticking, and overhead, in the apartment upstairs, it sounded as if someone were jumping rope.

Talk, Wendy had said. She always wanted to talk, but there were some things talk wouldn't fix. She wouldn't believe that. *Tell me, tell me what happened. Did something happen?*

Yes, and no, he'd say.

What's the yes part and what's the no part?

She said yes, and he said no. *Wendy, what's the use of talking? You either do it, or you don't.* And if you don't—if you *can't*—you might as well jump off a cliff!

He imagined her saying: Marcus, a one-time failure doesn't mean anything.

Maybe not to you, he would say.

Look, a little problem—

Little problem, he'd tell her. Can't you hear what you're saying? Don't you have any sensitivity? This wasn't a problem like an algebra problem where there was answer upside down in the back of the book. *This is my life. Forget it,*

Wendy, I'm giving up sex. Your loss! Then he'd give her a sad smile.

He saw himself the writer-hermit, but famous, and all the women who'd turned him down were begging him now. Oh, the sadness of life! He knew he was acting again, and then he thought of his father. Johnny Appleseed himself! He'd dropped his seed and ran off. Marcus had come into life an accident, an afterthought. He must never forget that.

When Sally and Bill came in, it was dark and still raining. Sally turned on a light. "Marcus, what are you doing sitting in the dark? Is something the matter?"

"Not at all," he said with quiet dignity.

"You should have come with us," Sally said. "We had the best time. Yelled ourselves hoarse for Sherwood."

Bill took a grapefruit from the refrigerator and started peeling it. "What did you do today?"

"Not much," Marcus said in the same somber tone. He didn't want to give up his subdued mood. Thoughtful, a little depressed. . . . Ah, Wendy, Wendybird, I flew from you, but I'll be back.

When he woke the next day he couldn't swallow and his head pounded. Still he tried to get up, mind over matter, but there was something the matter with his mind. His head wobbled, and felt like a pot of boiled potatoes. "Ma," he hollered for Sally, "I'm dying."

Sally stuck a thermometer under his tongue. A hundred and two degrees. He was a bona fide sickee. Sally fixed him up with two pillows and the TV at the foot of the bed. "Do you want to read? The light on? Do you want to watch TV?"

He could say yes and no and be grumpy, and just lie

there and stare at the ceiling, and not talk, or say anything that came into his head, and it was all right. He was sick, in pain; all was forgiven. Oh, Wendybird, do you know what's happened to me?

He slept a lot, most of the day, then slept the night through. In the morning, still feverish, he staggered to the bathroom, puked, took a shower, and changed his pajamas. He was in bed for four days. His grandmother came over with chicken soup in a jar. "You have this with noodles, and I guarantee you'll be out of bed tomorrow. Chicken soup and noodles go together like apple pie and graham crackers."

"Apple pie and ice cream, Grandma," Marcus said hoarsely.

"I get tired of hearing it that way. I like graham crackers and milk, don't you, darling?"

Alec came to see him. "Wendy told me you were at death's door." He smiled at himself in the mirror, then sat down on a chair next to the bed, took out his silver cigarette case. "Mind if I smoke?"

"Yes."

"How long are you going to stay in bed?"

"I may never get up, if I have to look at you."

"Oh, you're all right, there's nothing wrong with you. How's the writing going?" He lit a cigarette. "How's your sex life?"

"How's yours?"

"Comme ci, comme ca." Alec exhaled a stream of smoke. "I'm in a temporary fallow period. How are you and Wendy doing?"

"Okay."

"Too bad I let her go. She really liked me."

"Too bad you can't keep your mouth shut! Just stay away from Wendy and shut up about her."

Alec backed right off. "Sorry, comrade, I didn't know how sensitive and sick you were."

"Sick? You're sick! Just bug off, Canale. Wendy's not interested in you."

Alec put up his hands. "No problem, Comrade Marko-vitch. Forget I said anything."

"And don't call me comrade, you moron."

"Now you sound like yourself, Rosenbloom."

Marcus sank back against the pillow, surprised at himself. He'd pulled a real cave-man act. "Anyway, Wendy's too smart for you, Canale. You wouldn't know what to do with an honest-to-god smart woman."

22

"Stay home another day," Sally urged Marcus before she left for work Monday morning.

"Go ahead, I can take care of myself." He was definitely feeling better. "Quit hovering over me." He was full of resolutions. Time to take a more positive attitude toward life. Right now he was going to write, and later he was going to call Wendy.

Isabel Malefsky. He sat with his notebook open and thought about her. In Miss Black's sixth-grade class he'd sat behind Isabel feeling excited and aroused because of a girl for the first time in his life. He was still fat that year and shy around girls, and he never spoke to Isabel.

He remembered standing outside her window at night, dreaming that she would look out and see him.

He felt good writing it down. How fanatical, devoted, and dumb he'd been. On Valentine's Day he'd made a huge red heart out of construction paper. Inside he wrote, "Dear Is, Is you is, or is you ain't my valentine?" and signed it, "The Lone Ranger." He had taken the valentine to her house the night before Valentine's Day, slipped it under her door, then run for his life.

In class the next day, Isabel showed the valentine to everyone. "Did you send this stupid valentine? Did you? Did you?"

She stood in front of him, holding the valentine between two fingers as if it smelled. He shook his head. "It's you," she said. "I know it's you." She dropped it in the wastebasket. "It has to be a dumbbell like you."

Around three o'clock Marcus phoned Wendy. The phone rang several times before Wendy answered. "Hello," he said, "it's me."

"I'd never have known." Was there a coolness in her voice?

"You recognize my voice?"

"Unmistakable. Glad you got it back."

"What do you mean?" He was alarmed. Got what back?

"Don't you remember? Silent Sam. I was yapping away and you wouldn't talk."

"I was upset."

"I was, too, the way you were acting."

"I wasn't mad at you."

"Well, it sure seemed that way."

"What are you doing now?" he said. "Busy, I suppose? I know how it is when you're so popular."

"Yes, my fans are sooo demanding. They don't give me a minute's peace."

"Why don't you come over? Come up and see my aspirin sometime."

"What an irresistible offer. Do you mean it?"

"I want to see you, Wendy."

"In that case, I'm coming over."

Wendy was coming! He stretched out on the bed, then embraced the pillow. He had her in his arms, squeezing her tighter and tighter. "Wendy!" he shouted. Awww! His throat. "Wendy," he said more quietly. "Oh, Wendy." He kissed the pillow.

He got up, changed the sheets and pillowcase, took a shower, sprinkled himself with powder, dressed, and combed his hair. Ugh, too smooth! He messed it up again and lay back down on the bed.

He woke to hear Wendy in the other room talking to his mother. He sat up and rubbed his face, feeling suddenly tense and insecure. Wendy sounded so mature. Her voice, and the way she laughed—so sure and relaxed. Had she changed in these few days, found someone else?

"Hey, Wendy," he croaked, going into the living room. She wore shorts and clogs, her legs and arms brown and fit. She looked gorgeous. He put on a happy face. "How you doing?"

His mother felt his head. "I'm going out to meet Bill now. I'll be an hour, two at the most. Are you going to keep him company, Wendy?"

"If it's all right, Sally."

"Well, you're not going to catch anything. He's past the contagious period, but don't let him bully you."

"Cut it out, Sally."

His mother kissed him. "Try not to be as obnoxious to Wendy as you are with me."

"I'm never obnoxious to Wendy."

"I didn't realize how sick you were," Wendy said as they went to his room. "Sally was telling me. I should have come over sooner."

"You might have caught it."

"I wouldn't have cared. We could have been sick together."

In the same bed, he thought.

"You look a lot better than I expected," Wendy said.

"It's the company. It puts a bloom in my cheek and this croak in my voice." He sat on the edge of the bed. "Are you still mad at me?"

"I wasn't mad at you, Marcus. You were the one who was mad at me." She paced the room. "I tried to explain to you: with my uncle there, I just didn't feel right. And then you didn't say a word. I felt like such a fool. Yes, after *that*, I was sort of mad at you, I admit it."

"I wasn't mad at you either. I was mad at myself, the way things fizzled out."

"It wasn't the right place, I kept telling you."

"It was something else." He bit his lip. If she didn't know, should he say anything? Did she even still want to? "You don't know what happened, do you?"

"Yes I do. You got mad at me because I was making a fuss about the room being wrong."

"No, it wasn't you. *Me.* I tried, and I couldn't."

"Couldn't what?" She paused at the foot of the bed.

"I couldn't . . . He . . . That idiot! . . . *He wouldn't* . . . Understand?"

"Oh, was that it? What a misunderstanding. You were worried too. Not just me."

"Right."

"Sure, of course, I've read about that. They say ninety percent of sex is in the mind."

His hands were damp. He wanted her to sit on the bed, sit next to him, close. Did she still want to? "What're your thoughts about mental telepathy?" he asked.

"That's easy. Not very scientific."

"Watch this." Marcus put his fingertips to his temples. "I'm sending you a message. Do you receive my message?"

"Wait a minute, professor. What kind of message?"

"One you want to hear." He concentrated. *Do you want to? Do you want to? Do you?*

"Stop," Wendy cried, "I've got the message. You want . . . want . . . you want me to get on the bed next to you. Am I right?"

He moved over. "Close enough." She sat next to him, and they held hands.

"Now let's play another game," Wendy said. "Questions and answers. I ask and you answer. What do you think about me?"

"Can't you tell?"

"Don't answer a question with a question."

"I dreamed about you last night."

"What was the dream?"

"X-rated dream."

"Interesting?"

"Very."

"What did we do?"

"Well . . . something we wanted to do and didn't."

"I'm getting the picture, Swami."

She put her arm around his neck. They kissed then lay on the bed pressed close together. "You're going to get my cold," he said.

"I don't care. Isn't it nice being together again? I missed you."

"After last time, I was going to be a monk, give up sex, spend my life writing and making monk's bread."

"You're not the type. Let's take off some of these clothes. Do you want to?"

That had to be the dumbest question he'd ever heard.

"The door," Wendy said. He got up and pushed a chair under the knob. "Pull the shade," she said. "Do you think Sally will notice?"

"Sure. With her bionic vision, my mother notices everything."

"I'm serious. I wouldn't want her to know."

"Why? She'd love to have you in the family."

"Is that a proposal? Forget it. I'm not getting married for a long time."

He caught her hands. "Are we starting a fight?"

"No, let's start a kiss."

Holding hands, they kissed awkwardly. "We did better before," Wendy said. She pulled him down and leaned over him. After a while she said. "Marcus, do you think anybody's as slow and ignorant as we are?"

"I doubt it, but we'll get it." They kissed again, touched and kissed, and rolled around the bed. His breath was coming short. He fumbled, excited and scared. "Wendy, are you all right? . . . Should I? . . . Is it all right?"

"Yes, yes . . . please."

"We can stop anytime. Just say stop, and I'll stop. Do you want me to stop? I will, it doesn't matter."

"Stop talking so much, Marcus. I'm glad . . . yes . . ."

"Oh . . . Oh, Wendy, am I doing . . . is this right?"

"I think so. Yes, I think so . . . yes . . . okay . . . yes, yes, yes . . ." She was laughing. "It's so funny. My, god, Marcus, we're doing it!"

Later, with the shade up and the door open, they sat on opposite ends of the bed, looking at each other. Wendy had dealt out a hand of cards, but they weren't playing. "I think congratulations are in order," she said.

"Congratulations, Barrett."

"Congratulations, Rosenbloom."

23

The moment Marcus awoke the next morning he thought of what had happened—Oh, Wendy!—and he shouted with joy.

Outside his window the sparrows squabbled, traffic hummed, the world was waiting for him. He was up and out of bed, washed and dressed, not stopping for breakfast, banging down the stairs, bike on his shoulder. He wore an open-collared shirt, and a blue and white checked bandanna loosely knotted around his neck.

The bike purred along the road. Traffic was still light. He sniffed the fumes, a bracing smell of gas and oil. "Good morning," he said to a man who looked still half-asleep, dreaming about the her that he dreamed about. Marcus was on to everyone now. He'd found the key to the world's great secret. Everywhere people were doing it. Oh, joy!

He slowed to allow a young woman to cross in front of him. She hesitated, then stepped out quickly. Her feet in little blue and white sneakers seemed adorable to him. Don't be afraid of me, lovely lady. You can depend on Marcus.

Racing along with the cars, he felt comradely, friendly, a man among men. Yesterday he'd just been a kid with his tongue hanging out, but today, today, I am a man!

Wendy, wearing green Army fatigues, answered the door. "Marcus?" Why was she surprised to see him? "You're early. I'm still eating breakfast." She held up a spoon.

"I haven't eaten yet. I thought we could grab something together." Was that too raunchy? She was somehow different than he'd expected. Did she remember? She seemed so separate, cool, and distant, as if they'd just met.

Inside there was a dark pungent smell of coffee. Wendy's uncle in his white uniform was at the stove pouring himself a cup. He glanced at Marcus's bandana. "What's that? You got a sore throat?"

"Cornflakes?" Wendy said. "Milk, bananas? Your basic American breakfast. Help yourself, Marcus."

He was hungry, but uncomfortable with her uncle. The man's glance was keen, as if he'd guessed what Marcus was celebrating with the checked kerchief. "I'll wait for you outside, Wendy. Okay if I leave my bike here today?"

"Put it in the garage," Uncle Doug said, "so the kids don't play with it."

In the back the old apple tree was covered with fragrant blossoms. Marcus broke off a sprig.

"Isn't the tree beautiful?" Wendy propped her lunch and notebook between her knees and tied her hair back with a green kerchief.

He handed her the sprig of flowers. She wedged them into her notebook. "Let's go," she said.

He had expected more: deep lingering looks, a passionate kiss. "I haven't eaten yet," he said a little forlornly.

"You idiot, why didn't you eat when I asked you to?"

"Your uncle spooks me. You want to stop and get something?"

She looked at her watch. "We don't want to be late. Here, take my lunch."

He ate an egg salad sandwich and a banana. "I'll leave you the apple."

"No, eat it. I don't care. I'll buy something in school."

"Let me pay, then."

"Oh, forget it, what is it, a dollar? You paid for me lots of times."

He crumbled the empty bag and dropped it into a can. "Did you forget?" he said. Their eyes met.

"That's all I've been thinking about," she said. "I never thought I would feel this way. Isn't it funny, Marcus: here we are, the same people we were yesterday, but it's different. Do you feel it, too?"

"Yes," he said. "I feel different, the same but different."

"I thought I would feel good. You know, it's over with, I did it, hooray, and all that. But—" She linked arms with him. "I keep getting these weird, possessive thoughts. Like, he's mine, mine, mine!"

He smiled. "It's all right with me."

"Not with me. I don't want to own anyone. Just because we— No, I really didn't think it would be this way."

They held hands, lingering outside school, reluctant to separate. "You're right," he said, "people shouldn't belong to each other."

"Some people just hang on for dear life," Wendy said. "They make each other their security blankets. Some of the kids around school, the way they go around draped over each other, you'd need a crowbar to pry them apart." The bell rang.

"See you lunchtime," Marcus said.

"I can't. We're going on a botany field trip to Baltimore Woods."

"You mean I won't see you today?" He couldn't keep the disappointment from his voice.

"I'll stop by your house after school."

They separated near the gym. "Don't forget," he said, "I'll be waiting for you."

Lunchtime, outside, he moved languidly, the way he'd been moving all morning. No more speeding places, no more nervous gestures, no more yapping and jerking around every second. The new smooth Marcus, laid back, swinging his shoulders, free and easy. He smiled at several girls, really met their eyes.

In the shade, in front of the school, he sat on the railing with Pfeff, Gordy, and Alec. It was so hot everyone was out. Pfeff lit a cigar and Gordy sniffed appreciatively. "Umm, what we have here is the aroma of a fine panatella, a rich, earthy smell."

Pfeff held the cigar out. "That's not what it smells like."

"Don't say any more," Gordy warned, "or you will be expelled for poor English usage." Marcus's eyes followed the girls in brief shorts and tops going slowly past. Was he being disloyal to Wendy looking at other girls? Was she looking at guys the way he was looking at these girls? He didn't think he'd like it if she was.

Pfeff and Gordy were counting who had a bra on and who didn't.

"Bra," Pfeff said.

"Bouncer," Gordy said.

Marcus turned to Alec. "How's Terri these days? Don't hear you talk about her much."

"She's gone to California, to see her father."

"You're all alone. That's sad."

Alec shrugged. "She'll be back this summer."

"I'm thinking of traveling this summer." Marcus reknotted the scarf around his neck. "Going up to Canada, to Algonquin Park, or maybe out west."

"Hey, Marc, I'll go with you." Pfeff talked around his cigar.

"Not if you smoke those things. I've got my partner anyway. A lot better looking than you."

"You're going to travel with a girl?" Pfeff spit. "Horseballs, right? Who is she? You don't have a girl."

Marcus sat back. Alec was listening. "It's still in the early planning stages."

"That means you haven't even talked to her?" Pfeff said.

"Oh, we're *talking*, all right." He knocked his pipe out on the railing, then stood up. "Lots of talk." He clapped Alec on the back. "See you guys. I've got a busy afternoon."

It was hot in the house, airless. He stripped down to his shorts and sat by the open window with his notebook. Idly he titled the Isabel story, "A Dumbbell Like You."

Later he moved one of his mother's big plants from the living room to his room. If Wendy came too late, nothing would happen. He was practical and dreamy, and full of plans. When she came in he'd catch her in his arms, carry her to the bed, and then . . . ? He couldn't imagine how they'd managed it; the whole thing now seemed extraordinary. This bed. In this very bed! He thought of all the places he'd heard or read about people doing it: the kitchen table, in the bathtub, in elevators, on roofs, even in airplanes.

The bell rang. "Hello." Wendy's face was flushed, her shirt out. There was a dandelion tangled in her hair.

"Inside all this time! How can you stand it? It's so gorgeous out." She handed him a blue-jay feather. "I've got to have something to drink."

In the kitchen he poured her a glass of milk and told her the Isabel story. "Poor Marcus, I would never have been so cruel." She leaned her cheek against his.

He put his arm around her. "Story time is over." He looked into her eyes. "What do you want to do now?" *I want to go to bed with you.*

She fanned her face. "It's so close in here."

"How's it outside?" he said. *Let's take off our clothes.*

"Oh, not bad. Want to go out?"

"Do you?" *We could take a shower together.*

"Maybe we could find someplace cool."

"Let's try the roof," he said.

On the roof, heat beat up from the tar. The light was blinding. A line of clothes snapped in the wind. It looked like the worst place to escape from the heat, but on the shaded side of the elevator shaft it was cooler. And there, as if it were waiting for them, was a faded old mattress.

"Look what some kind person has left us," Marcus said. He stooped down and felt it. "Dry too."

"I don't believe this," Wendy said. "Where did it come from?"

"Got me, but aren't you glad?"

"You knew it was here all the time."

"I'm as surprised as you." He fell on the mattress. "Comfortable, though. Try it. The breeze is great here."

Wendy sat down next to him. "Is this where you bring all your girls?"

He tickled her neck. "A dumbbell like me?"

"Funny, Rosenbloom."

He leaned toward her, and they kissed. "How come you're smiling so much?" she said.

They kissed again. "I hope nobody comes up here," Wendy said.

"I'm listening. My bat ears will hear them coming six flights down. We are alone."

"We'd better be." She half rolled on top of him, kissed him on the mouth, then rolled herself all over him.

Afterward he remembered the snapping sheets, and the smell of tar and clean laundry, and the musty mattress, and how sticky they were.

24

The next time they went back to the roof, a woman was there with her children, hanging up clothes. She gave them a long suspicious look, and then went away. The next time, the mattress was gone.

After school on Friday, Wendy came over to the house and they went straight to Marcus's room and shut the door. Bill walked in almost on their heels. "There goes a beautiful idea," Wendy said.

Marcus opened the door. "Hello, Bill. Wendy's here."

"How are you kids doing?" Bill removed his tie. "Did Sally tell you what she wanted to do about supper, Marc?"

"No idea." Bill went to see if there was a note in

the kitchen. "Shut the door," Marcus said.

"We can't. Bill's here."

"I know it. I want to have a temper tantrum." He could hear Bill whistling in the kitchen.

"Don't worry about it," Wendy said. "He's here, so we've just got to change gears."

"I don't feel like a car," Marcus said. "I want to throw things." He picked up Wendy's sneakers and threw them into the closet. Then a magazine, then the blanket from the foot of bed, then the pillow. "And now the mattress. Off the bed, Wendy."

She got up. "Go ahead. Get it out of your system." She helped him drag the mattress off the bed. "Why don't you throw your desk out the window?" She made him laugh finally.

At supper they sat with Sally and Bill. The four of them together was kind of dull, but cozy and domestic. Bill talked about diets, and Sally agreed with everything he said. "You just can't eat as much as you get older, not if you want to stay in shape."

Marcus yawned. "Come on, you guys, I hate it when you get going like this. These two are so self-satisfied," he said to Wendy. He was the first one done eating. "You're a poke," he said, putting his arm across Wendy's chair. "How come you walk so fast and eat so slow? Hurry up." Then he pulled her chair away from the table and grabbed her under the arms. "You've eaten enough. You'll get fat as a cow. Let's go. I know where we can get some really good hot fudge sundaes."

"You're leaving the cleanup to us?" Sally said.

"Sure, what else do you two old folks have to do?"

"Ha ha, very funny. Bill did the whole supper. He told me you didn't lift a finger. Now you do the cleanup."

"How about you?" Marcus said.

"I supervise."

"Do I get the car then?"

Sally looked at Bill. "Are we doing anything?"

"There's a Clint Eastwood movie at the James."

"You'd go to a Clint Eastwood movie?" Marcus said. "Ugh!"

"I love Clint Eastwood," Wendy said. "What's wrong with that?"

Marcus pulled her aside and whispered. "Will looking at his manly torso make you so sexy you won't be able to keep your hands off me?"

"Not unless there's a full moon," Wendy said.

By the time the dishes were done Sally and Bill had decided to stay home, so Marcus got the car. He and Wendy drove around for a while. It was hard to find a decent place to park. A lot of places like down along the railroad tracks, or in back of the Field House, were just too creepy. One night they'd driven around for an hour and couldn't find anything. Tonight, Marcus pulled in back of a dark gas station between a couple of wrecked cars. It smelled greasy. He ran his hand lightly up Wendy's arm, lingering at her bra strap. She wriggled her shoulders. "What do you think?"

"Stinks."

"You never think of places," he said. "You just turn them down."

"Oh, this place is *perfect*," Wendy said. "Don't you just love the smell of old greasy oil?"

"Do you have a better suggestion?"

Wendy stuck her head out the window. "Look, Marcus, there's the Big Dipper, and that's the North Star. Do you know any of the constellations? Look, I think that one— see those stars in a row—that's Berenice's Hair."

He pulled her back into the car. "What do you see now?"

"A big, dark, doggy head."

"Woof, woof." He kissed her, and unbuttoned her shirt.

"What are you doing, Marcus?"

"Guess."

"Marcus, let's just talk for a while."

He heard her, but he didn't hear her. He felt like it. He always felt like it! He got his hand under her knees and pulled her next to him.

She shook free. "What is this caveman approach?"

"I thought you were in the mood for Clint Eastwood?"

"You don't look like Clint Eastwood to me."

"What's the matter, am I especially repulsive tonight?"

"I just feel like talking for a while."

"Okay, go ahead, talk." He grinned, but he felt cheated and belligerent. He put his hands behind his head, didn't look at her, and started whistling.

"You're sulking," she said.

"Not me. I'm whistling."

"Do we have to be making it every second? Is that the only reason we hang out? For that one reason only?"

"No! If you don't want to, I don't want to. I don't care."

"Don't be reckless, Marco." They kissed. "You know," she said, "there are times when I don't want to."

"Then you shouldn't." They kissed again. No rush. Nice

guys didn't push. But all the time they were saying how open and frank they'd always be, he kept hoping that his Mr. Nice Guy sincerity would pay off.

A police cruiser slid around the corner and turned its spotlight on them.

"Oh, no!" Wendy exclaimed.

It was a good thing they were still sitting in the front seat. The cop got out of his car, the shiny black bulge of his gun in Marcus's face. "Let's see your license. Registration too." Marcus felt grim, stupid, like a kid who'd been caught doing something. Wendy didn't say a word.

"Whose car is this?"

"My mother's."

"Does she know you're here?"

"Does my mother know I'm here!"

"Listen, this is private property. I catch you here again, I'm going to run you and your cutie in."

The cop waited till Marcus backed out and drove away, then followed them for several blocks. Marcus had a red-hot coal in his stomach.

"Let's go home," Wendy said.

"Why? He shouldn't have bothered us. We weren't doing anything."

"We might have been, Marcus. That would have been nice."

"I think that's what he was hoping for. Cops are like anyone else, sneaking around trying to see what they aren't supposed to."

"Oh, I don't know," Wendy said. "It *was* private property."

"Have you noticed that you have an answer for everything!" He drove down behind some stores, but it was all wrong after that.

"We'd better call it quits." Wendy said.

"No, we're not."

"Why are you so belligerent?"

"Because I'm male."

"Then be less male."

"I bet you'd love that."

He kept looking for a place that would satisfy Wendy. Any place would have satisfied him.

"We're not going to find anyplace."

"Yes, we are."

He finally parked at the end of a dead end street, with a lot of overhanging trees. There were a few houses nearby, but it was dark and quiet and there was no traffic. "What do you think? This is perfect."

"I told you I don't think we should park at all. I'm really nervous now."

He put his arms around her. "You know you don't mean that." He teased her a little. "I'll protect the little cutie."

"Ugh!" She dug her elbow into his ribs. "I hate that word."

He kissed her. She put her arms around his neck. He began to feel good again. It was going to happen, and he felt warm, eager, and helpful. "Let's get in back. Here, I'll give you a hand."

"I'm not an old lady." She looked out the window. "I think I see somebody."

"Nobody's out there."

"Marcus, we're right in front of a house."

"Listen to how quiet it is." There was a glow in the

distance, but around them was an island of dark. "It's perfect, I tell you."

"And I tell you tonight is jinxed. It's late, too, with all this driving around."

"You're just working me up, aren't you? Saying yes and then no."

She swung around. "What does that mean?"

"Feminine wiles," he said. "A little resistance makes the game more exciting." He understood her perfectly. It was like a dance: he advanced, and she retreated.

"Feminine wiles? Me! Wendy Barrett using feminine wiles." She laughed. "This really is incredible, Marcus. If it wasn't so funny it would be stupid!"

"Then get in back with me," he ordered.

"I'm not playing games, Marcus."

He climbed into the front seat, had the impulse to bite her, and kissed her hard.

She pulled back. "This is really bad. Why do you put on so much pressure? It used to be fun. Now I feel there's only one thing on your mind. Do it, do it, do it! Like a couple of monkeys."

"That's right." He could have been clever and denied it was true, but he was too angry. "Sex is what I'm thinking about. You're thinking about it too," he said.

"Yes, but not every minute!"

She was so righteous. "That's a lot of bull. You never minded before. It's the end, isn't it. A change in policy. It's the Cold War again. Say it, Wendy. Quit crapping around and say it."

"What are you talking about? The *end?* Why is it always the end with you? Every time we have an argument, it's the end, the *end.*"

Shut up, he muttered to himself. He started the engine and spun the car around. He didn't realize how out of control he was. He misjudged the width of the road and scraped the curb. It sounded as if the whole side of the car was being ripped open. He jumped out and ran around the side of the car, but couldn't see anything. Wendy got out, too. He felt the rough place where the paint had been scraped off.

"That's it," he said. "That's the end. Once Sally sees this, I'll never get the car again."

"It's not that bad," Wendy said. "Just some paint. Tell her you'll pay to have it fixed."

It was this whole stinking evening. Running around like rabbits, then the cop, then fighting with Wendy, and now this. "Let's go home," he said.

"No," she said, "let's make up. The whole evening's been a downer. Let's do something we like. You want to?"

"I don't care."

"I do. Let's go to the Pie Shop."

A movie crowd filled the restaurant, but they found a table in back. There was a gang of shrieking kids at a nearby table.

"What do you think of this place?" Wendy said. "Do you think this is a good place to make out?"

He looked around. "I don't know."

"Perfect!" Wendy said, mocking Marcus.

They both started to giggle. He reached under the table and rubbed her knees.

They were friends again, that was easy, but he was right about the car. There was no more borrowing his mother's car after that evening.

25

Wendy and Marcus decided to bike out to Green Lake early on Memorial Day so they could spend the day together, before Marcus went to work. He'd been working for more than a week now at Nadia's Market, part-time, from four in the afternoon to nine at night.

It was a perfect day, not a cloud in the sky. Marcus had rolled his bathing suit and towel in a small blanket, and on the way they stopped and bought a long Italian bread, milk, cheese, and pickles. Wendy wanted Sicilian black olives, and Marcus, a frozen Sara Lee chocolate cake. Early as it was, the park was crowded, so after they swam they climbed up the hill, leaving their bikes chained below.

"Remember the Isabel story?" Marcus said. "Sweeny liked it and gave it to a friend of his on the newspaper, who's an editor. Maybe they'll publish it in the weekend supplement."

"When will you know?" Wendy said. "Call me the minute you find out."

They set out their blanket on top of the hill near a clump of cedars, then unpacked the food. The pickles were sour, the milk warm, and the chocolate cake runny, but they ate everything except a little bit of the cake and bread.

"This is a good place," Marcus said. "Good" being a euphemism.

"Good," Wendy agreed. "Private. Nice."

They wrapped up in the blanket. He was eager; it had been a while. Hidden under the blanket, they kissed. Marcus unhooked Wendy's bikini. They peeked out, and went under the blanket again. "If anyone comes," Wendy said, "we'll tell them we're changing the film in the camera."

Afterward they finished the last of the cake and bread. Marcus had his head in Wendy's lap, looking up at the sky. Wendy pinched his cheeks and kissed him. "Umm, I like those cute chubby cheeks."

He must have slept, because when he woke the sky had begun to cloud. Lines of luscious fat clouds bumped each other like fat thighs and breasts. He began to daydream about Karen. Nothing serious. He'd be strolling around, and they'd meet. He'd have his shirt open, some beads around his neck, showing a lot of chest, a soft fedora hat cocked over one eye . . .

She'd come up . . . see him . . . He'd look her right in the eyes, a suggestive look, a look that would tell her everything. *He knew.* None of those men she hung around with knew any more than he did. He'd just touch her arm and then he'd walk off. That's all.

"What are you smiling about?" Wendy said, stroking his head.

"Karen," he said and knew the minute he said it that it had been a mistake. He made it worse explaining. "I was just daydreaming, what if I ran into her?" He said too much. "It's a funny idea, isn't it?"

"How often do you think about Karen?"

"I never think about her."

"Marcus! You've just been thinking about her!"

"Okay, sometimes."

"When?"

"I don't know. What are you getting so mad about?"

"Do you think about her when we're doing it?"

"No, no!"

"You do, don't you?"

"No!"

"I'm just a substitute for Karen to you."

"It's not true."

"What if I told you I'm dreaming about Alec, going up to him and letting him know that anytime he's interested . . . Would you think that's just a little funny daydream?"

"Are you thinking about him?"

"No! I'm thinking about you." Her eyes filled with tears. She broke away, looked for a tissue, then wiped her eyes on the blanket.

"I thought you'd laugh." He defended himself lamely, aware that he was still saying the wrong thing. "Listen, I'm sorry," he said. "Let's forget it." He tried to put his arm around her, but she pushed him away.

"Don't. *Don't.* Just leave me alone. I don't want to be pawed, Marcus. You don't own me."

"I never said I did."

"But that's what you think."

He couldn't get things straight. Whatever he said only made it worse. It was like falling down a slippery chute, going down and down. He couldn't stop himself.

"You don't care about me," she said. "It's just *lie down!* Everytime you come around—Lie down!" She jumped up, left him there on the hill, and ran back to the beach. By the time he came down she was gone, and so was her bike.

He saw Wendy a few times in school, but she avoided him. When he called her, she was always "busy" or "out" or would "call back." What was going on? So they had had a dumb little fight. They'd had fights before. What he'd said was so trivial, a slip. It didn't mean what she thought it did. He was determined to speak to her, and went over to her house, one afternoon, before going in to work.

Wendy was there, on the side lawn, swinging a couple of kids. She was bareheaded, her hair fluffed out and full of light. He hesitated. What was the best approach? Casual? Act like nothing had happened? Or be straightforward, get right to the point. *Wendy, you're making a mountain out of a molehill!*

"There's Marcus," one of the kids yelled. Wendy glanced around.

"Hi," he said, approaching, smiling, swinging his shoulders, full of bravado, but somewhat worried, unsure of how she'd react.

"Hi," she said, as if she'd just swallowed a fly.

Marcus leaned on the bars of the swing set. "How's it going?"

"Okay."

"You watching all these kids? Where's your aunt? How come you don't answer the phone?"

"When?"

"I called you the other day. Why didn't you call me back?"

"I don't remember."

"Sally wants you to come over and eat some night."

She gave him a look. He talked but she wasn't helping him. It made everything he said sound empty, like a lot of blah-blah, as if he were trying to blow up a balloon with a hole in it. The minute he stopped talking he felt the balloon collapse. "Want to do something Saturday?"

"No." She gave the little girl in the swing a push.

"Want me to swing her a while?"

"No."

Here he was trying to make up their quarrel. What did she want? What was the matter with her?

"Why not? Come on." He pushed her, gave her an angry, aggressive, confident grin. "Let a man do this." He was going to make her talk to him whether she wanted to or not. He pushed the swing. "Whee! We're not still having an argument, are we? I'm not mad."

"Bully for you."

"Are you still mad?"

"No."

"Good." He smiled. "And since I'm not mad, either, we've made up."

"Oh, Marcus, don't be simpleminded!"

That stung. "Listen, what's the matter? You *are* still mad, aren't you? About that Karen business . . ."

"I'm not thinking about that anymore," Wendy said thinly.

"Good," he said, though he didn't believe her. "I thought maybe you were still brooding over it."

"I never *brooded* over it. I didn't like it, and I told you so. Stacy, you stop fighting with Meredith. Either play with her nicely or get out of the sandbox." She pushed Marcus aside and went back to swinging the little girl.

Marcus's eyes went angrily to the peak of the house. "Why don't you admit it, Wendy? You're still pissed. You say you aren't, but you are."

"Not true." She stopped pushing the child. "I'm not mad about anything, Marcus. I just don't care to go out."

"Higher," the girl in the swing screamed. "Higher, Wendy!"

"Any particular reason?" He felt like grabbing her and yelling in her face. "Any special reason you don't want to do anything?" he asked again.

"Yes."

"Are you busy Saturday?"

"No."

"So?"

"Marcus, you *know* why. Don't make me repeat it. It comes down to a question of sex. That's what our friendship's all about: sex, and little else."

"Not true," he said. Unfair. They *were* friends. It wasn't just sex. He wasn't here just to get her back in the sack with him. That was wrong. Why did she keep harping on it? "That isn't the only thing we do."

"No?" She laughed mockingly. "Why else are you here now, Marcus?"

"Because I like you and I want to make up our fight."

"Like me for what? Don't be a hypocrite."

"It *isn't* that."

"It is, it always is."

"Oh, shit." He walked away, sat in the sandbox with a little boy, and helped him make a sand mountain.

When he looked around, Wendy was calling the children together. Her aunt came out of the house with a tray of milk and cookies. "Hello, Marcus," she called cheerfully, "You want a cookie too?" Wendy passed out the straws. Marcus pulled her to one side. "I know what you're getting at, but it's not that way. It really isn't. We do things. It isn't just *that*."

She handed out the last of the straws. "When's the last time we just sat around, had fun the way we used to at the mall, or in the park, just watching people, doing nothing?"

"We can do that again. We don't have the time."

"Right, that's it. We don't have the time for anything but—"

He wanted to prove to her how wrong she was. "I could have told Alec about us," he said, "and I didn't." It sounded stupid even to him.

"You want a medal?" she said.

He threw up his hands. "Oh, forget it! I'm just trying to tell you something. It's not only sex. I've got some feelings, too!"

"Oh, sure, you've got your head in my lap and you're getting off on a little fantasy about Karen. That's really tender."

"Karen was *nothing*. She wanted a baby-sitter. Nothing happened."

"But you wanted something to happen. Don't act dense, Marcus. It's all gotten down to one thing." She kept her voice low. "Almost from the minute we began, that's all it's been. I'm sorry now we ever started. Sex is not a good enough reason for sex."

"What does that mean? It doesn't make sense." She was so hard and self-righteous. It made him want to retaliate. "You're so sure that's what I want. Maybe I'm not interested in you that way, anymore!"

"Okay," she said, giving him a proud look. "That's fine with me."

"This time it's the end, right?" He felt this was the moment she'd been waiting for. "You got what you wanted, I got what I wanted; it's even steven."

"Yes," she said. "I think we should stop seeing each other."

"Stop seeing each other?" He was totally unprepared. "Why don't you quiet down?" he said. It wasn't his voice, but it was him speaking. The voice, the words, seemed to come from a distance. "Quiet down," he repeated. "Quiet down!" He was trembling, he felt so bad. "Quiet down!" he said, and then he walked away.

26

Some days were good, some not so good, some awful. Sometimes Marcus felt as if he'd been hit in the head. He missed Wendy. He saw her in school sometimes, at the graduation rehearsals. She saw him, too, but they never spoke.

The weather changed. A grayness descended on the city. There was a grayness in him, too. Nothing seemed important, or exciting, or worth doing. He went along from day to day, did all the things he said he would do. He was actually more disciplined and in a better routine than he'd ever been, but nothing seemed to matter very much.

One day, passing by Burger King, he saw Wendy and Alec sitting together. She had her head down and he was rubbing her neck. Marcus moved by fast, then went back and looked again. It was them, Wendy and Alec together. They didn't even see him looking.

It made him want to kick something. At home, he kicked the wall. A little mirror his mother had left on the hall table fell and cracked. He looked down, saw his face in the mirror, part in one half, part in the other. That was the way he felt: split apart, half of him furious, half of him abject and sorry.

Marcus was at work at Nadia's, a few days later, when Bev Kruger, wearing a yellow sunsuit, came into the market. It was a hot, sticky afternoon, and the plastic shades were drawn against the sun. "Oh, hi!" Bev was surprised to see him, but not pleasantly. He rang up her order crisply: a couple of energy bars, macaroons, a box of Fig Newtons, Fritos, a six-pack of Coke. He wore a tie and green jacket. Captain Nadia ran a trim, neat ship. He handed her the total. She paid. He snapped open a paper bag and started packing. They had nothing to say to each other.

"Who's got the sweet tooth?" he said.

"Oh, that." Bev smiled vaguely. "We're on our way to a picnic. It's been so hot today. It's not bad here."

"Good air conditioning."

"It must be hard when you go out."

"Hate to leave the job," he agreed. He was smiling a lot, trying to impress her. He remembered to ask about her sister in the hospital. "That must be rough, having to wear a brace all the time."

"My sister's home now." Bev stood there and talked to him, picking up her package a couple of times, then

169

putting it down. *Are you watching, Wendy? See me talking to Bev Kruger?*

Bev lingered. How long could he hold her here? No longer Marcus the madman. This was Marcus the honest workman, sincere, safe, interested, appreciative . . . *Wendy, do you see how well I do this?* Bev had always drawn him, that speckled juiciness. Not like Wendy, not playful, not joshing—not at all like Wendy, but nice, very nice. *Lots of nice girls in the world besides you, Wendy Barrett.*

Oh, be honest, Marcus. It was Wendy in his head, disagreeing as always.

Okay, so I am thinking about you, still thinking about you. Only I don't want to, and I don't have to. Bev is one attractive girl.

"It's hard to believe we're graduating in a few days," Bev said. "It feels like I just started Sherwood yesterday."

"I know," he said.

"Last year I was just a kid and now . . . You change so fast, it's a little scary sometimes. Well." She picked up her package. "I really better go."

He followed Bev in her yellow sunsuit. Not yet, but maybe soon. She was someone he might want when he got Wendy out of his head. *Do you hear me, Ms. Barrett?*

On Monday, after his exam, he got a phone call. "Mr. Rosenbloom?"

For a moment he thought it was Wendy playing a joke on him the way she used to. "The one and only," he said, suddenly happy. "Is that you, Wendybird?"

"This is Eileen Sabine at the *Morning Standard*, Mr.

Rosenbloom. Ted Sweeny sent me a story of yours about a valentine. We'd like to publish it in the weekend supplement. Would you mind if we bought it now and held it till next Valentine's Day? I know it's a long time. And we can only pay twenty-five dollars. Is that all okay?"

"Yes, thank you very much."

It took him a while to absorb the news. His first acceptance; his first published story. He'd been down so long, he had to tell himself to be happy. "Zowee," he murmured. "You're going to be a published writer. Zowee!" *Don't jump around like a kid. Show some dignity.* He put his head out the window. "Zowee!" Then he really got into it and gave the world a true Rosenbloom Salute. "Zoweeeeeeeeeee!"

"Hello? Wendy?"

"This is her aunt."

"This is Marcus. I have to talk to Wendy."

"She's not here right now, Marcus."

"Where is she? I've got to talk to her right away."

"She's taking her American History finals. I'll have her call you when she comes in."

"Hello, Wendy?" He called her again at suppertime, speaking quickly, urgently. "I've got to see you. It's important."

"What is it? Can't you tell me over the phone?"

"No, it's too important. I want to tell you face to face."

"Marcus, I think we said it all. There's no point—"

"It's not *that*. This is something else. You're going to like this." She finally agreed to meet him at the Rite Aid

Drugstore on Westcott. "Be there at seven-thirty, on the button," Marcus said.

"I'll try," she said. "I don't have a lot of time. I have an exam tomorrow."

He was there promptly at seven-thirty, but it was almost eight before he saw her coming. He'd pushed their disagreements out of his mind. He felt his news—he'd sold a story!—would somehow solve everything.

He had planned to build it up. He'd ask her to go someplace and sit down, and then he'd tell her, a little bit at a time. But the minute he saw her he blurted it out. "I had a story accepted. The editor called me today. I wanted you to be the first to know." He caught her hand.

"That's wonderful, Marcus. Is it the story about the valentine?" She pulled free. "You're going to see your story in print, your name in lights." She was saying the right things, but . . .

The exuberance went out of him.

"It's just a newspaper, the local rag." What about us, he wanted to say. "You want to get something to eat?"

"No, I'd better go back."

He'd said too much, been too excited. Wendy had been polite, that's all. "I saw you with Alec." He didn't even want to think about it, just said it to torture himself.

"When was that?"

She couldn't remember all the times. "In Burger King."

"Oh, that."

Now she was going to tell him nothing. "Are you and he friends again?"

"We've been talking."

"Talking!" He was sneering and he didn't give a damn.

"Isn't it cute, Alec, what I did with Marcus? Did you tell him about the ring on your finger? Or did you tell him you put it through my nose?"

"Oh, god!" she said.

He didn't say anything else, just walked the last blocks to her house in silence. "Well," she said in front of her house, "I'm really happy about your story. Good night, Marcus."

Dear Cool, Calm, and Collected
(AKA Wendy Barrett),

I don't know why I'm writing to you. I know that nothing I say will influence you. You were like ice when I saw you. What will convince you that I'm the way I've always been? My feelings haven't changed. I like us, it's not just sex, but you won't believe that. Your mind is made up. I've never met anyone so stubborn.

What we had was right and good. How can I think it's perfect while you hate it? You've never explained that to me. I don't think you can.

Do you know the female spider who uses the male for her own satisfaction, then devours him?

Dear Black Widow Spider, I am ready to throw myself into your sticky net again. Spider Lady . . . Spider Face . . . Oh, Wendy, you spider! Take your face away and leave me alone.

This is a crazy letter. I'll tear it into small pieces and put it into an envelope and slip it under your door. Then you can put it together like a jigsaw puzzle, piece by piece, so you'll know the way I feel.

You say I have sex on the brain. I don't deny it. When I see you, I want you. I did the other night. Is that wrong? Maybe I shouldn't feel this way all the time, but you're wrong if you think that's the only thing I feel.

You probably don't believe this. You think I'm exaggerating again. Rosenbloom, the story teller. If it is a story, it must be a good one. There are tears in my eyes.

How can I make you believe me?

How can I prove that I mean what I say?

I liked us!

Good-bye, Wendy . . .

27

The seniors were lined up alphabetically outside the auditorium in their white caps and gowns. Marcus was toward the back, Pfeff in front of him. He flipped up his gown and showed Marcus his No Nukes shorts. Twirling his cap on his finger, Marcus tried to spot Wendy at the front, but it was hard to distinguish anybody in all this white. He saw Alec, but only because Alec turned and waved.

There was a ripple of excitement down the corridor as the central doors of the auditorium were opened. Marcus planted the cap squarely on his head as the school band started a slow, solemn march. In two long lines the seniors shuffled down the center aisle of the darkened auditorium.

Before them was the lighted stage, around them the glittering sound of the band, ahead of them the principal, teachers, and other dignitaries awaiting their approach. In the audience parents, relatives, and friends turned their faces toward the seniors.

Marcus looked around. This would be the last time he walked down this familiar aisle. *It will never be the same again.* The thought came with unexpected force. He had resisted the sentiment of graduation: the ceremony, the solemnity, even pretentiousness. Only now, for the first time, he felt its truth and importance.

They moved into the reserved seats at the front of the auditorium, and on a signal sat down as one. Marcus turned his face to the stage, glad that he was here, and that Sally had fought with him and kept him from dropping out of school altogether. And again he looked for Wendy, this time finding her. She was facing forward, and he could only see her profile, and her hair pushed out around the cap—those familiar but so distant features. She was so far from any thought of him. Why was he still thinking about her when she was oblivious to him?

The moment of graduation was swift. Names were called out. Judith Aronson. Gordon Bruce. Marcus looked out over the filled auditorium, the rows of faces. Sally and Bill were there somewhere, his grandmother. Perhaps his father? Marcus hadn't written to tell him, and Sally never would, but still the thought had come.

Harmony. Kemper. Pfefferblitt. Finally, his name. He walked across the stage, accepted his diploma, received a quick, hard handshake from the distinguished personage, then he was off the stage. That was it.

After the ceremony he stood with his mother in the bright sunlight in front of the school while Bill took their picture with his Polaroid. "Hi, everyone." It was Wendy.

Sally hugged her. "Congratulations!"

"Thank you. You're all invited to a party my Aunt Ginny is giving."

"Wonderful. And I was feeling guilty about not making a party for Marcus."

"My mother's coming. She's flying in this afternoon."

"Then I wouldn't miss it for the world," Sally said. "Bill take a picture of the three of us. Here, Marcus, you in the middle."

It was hard for him to stand next to Wendy. "Closer," Bill said. "Marcus, put your arms around the girls."

He balanced the weight of his arm so it barely lay on her shoulder. "Sorry," he murmured. He felt nothing from her. She stood beside him cool and remote. He was the fool for feeling what he did. The moment the picture was taken she stepped aside, but stayed till the picture was developed.

Several times he caught her looking at him but each time he returned the look she glanced away. She surprised him when she asked if he wanted to come to her aunt's house early and help set up for the party. At first he wasn't even sure she was talking to him, she spoke so indifferently, as if whatever he did meant nothing to her one way or the other. Well, he could be as cool as she was.

"Sure," he said. "I'm not doing anything." But the roughness in his voice betrayed him. He wasn't cool, couldn't be cool near her.

In the picture, when it was finally developed, Marcus

stood a head taller than either Sally or Wendy, the tassel of his cap hanging over his nose.

"Will you get the horses down from the loft in the garage," Ginny said to Marcus later that afternoon. "How does it feel being a high-school graduate?"

"Good," Marcus said. "Maybe a little strange."

"I know, I still remember my high-school graduation, believe it or not, and that is strange. Wendy, you want to help Marcus?"

They carried the horses out onto the grass, then went back to get the boards. "Good weather for a party," he said.

"Terrific."

"Do you want me to hose down the boards," he called to Ginny in the house. "They're awfully dusty."

"Good idea, but don't get water over everything."

"Don't worry," Marcus said, "I'm a high-school graduate." Wendy smiled. Marcus ran the hose over the planks, and she wiped them down. The more he relaxed, the more he was aware of how almost formal they were with each other. Another time he would have sprayed her accidentally on purpose, and they would have fought over the hose.

"What did you think of the graduation?" he said.

"I liked it, but I felt sort of out of it. I kept thinking about my friends in Buffalo who are graduating."

"That's tough," he agreed. "Did you see what Pfeff was wearing under his graduation gown?" She shook her head. "His No Nukes shorts. I was waiting for him to flash them when he was on the stage."

"That would have livened things up."

They strung lanterns and lights along the porch, and out to the swings, and back to the corner of the house. Marcus held the ladder while Wendy hung the lights. "I suppose we're still friends," he said.

Wendy looked down from the ladder. "I suppose we are."

And he couldn't keep himself from saying, "The way we were: that's over then?"

She hesitated, hooked a light over the wire, then nodded. "Yes, that's over."

Later, when he went home to change he almost didn't go back to the party. Every time he saw Wendy, he began to hope, and then afterward he felt the way he felt now. Sally, though, wouldn't hear of his not going. "No, Marcus, Grace wants to see you. And Bill and I want to go. What would we be celebrating without you there?"

That night at the party there were some kids he knew and some he didn't know. Doug had set the stereo speakers in the living room windows and people were dancing on the grass. The horses and boards had been covered with white sheets and were laden with cold cuts, rye bread and rolls, pickles and relishes, a pot of baked beans, and a pan of Aunt Ginny's special chili.

Wendy, her hair caught with a ribbon, brought out more food. She was barefoot, wearing a long peasant skirt, and carried a tray from group to group, smiling, talking to everyone, offering them food. She had something for everyone but nothing for him.

Turn around, he commanded. It was a message from his head to hers, like the mental telepathy game they'd once played—it seemed ages ago—when they had only to look into each other's eyes to know. *Turn around, Wendy.* If she turned and looked at him it would prove they were still on the same wave length. But she remained untouched, or if she heard, unmoved.

He strolled around with his pipe in one hand, beer in a paper cup in the other. There were people all over the lawn, chairs turned over, paper plates and cups. His mother and Grace were sitting talking on the porch, Bill and another man on the railing nearby.

Grace was, as always, dazzling, her blond hair in a bun, wearing gold hoops in her ears. He had adored her when he was younger, thought she was the most beautiful woman in the world, and he still admired her.

"Marcus, my dear! I haven't seen you in so long. You've grown. Sally warned me. Now tell me, how tall are you?"

"Seven or eight feet."

"Marcus!" She pinched his cheek. "Wendy tells me that you've written a wonderful story, and that it's going to be published."

He smiled, remnants of his old pleasure and embarrassment near Grace still clinging to him.

Wendy came up behind him. "Cookies, anyone?"

"I don't dare," Grace said.

"Have a cookie, Marcus," Wendy said.

He held up his paper cup. "Beer and cookies don't mix." They walked along together. "I'm feeling let down," he said, "Do you feel it?"

"Graduation blues," she said.

"Something's over that will never return."

"Sentimental."

"That's me." He felt the emptiness of their conversation.

This is the way it would be when they met from now on. They'd smile and say meaningless things. He'd said they were friends, insisted on it, and she'd agreed. Yes, they were friends, but not the way they'd been friends in the beginning, or afterward either. Maybe Wendy was right: sex had come between them, poisoned their friendship. He didn't like to think so, didn't like that idea at all! But did it matter anymore what he liked or believed? Whatever they'd had, friendship or sex, friendly sex or sexy friendship, it was gone now. It was as if a crack had opened in the bottom of the sea, and what was warm, brimming, and vital had all drained away.

He was surprised to see Alec and Helen Wing. They came late. Alec embraced Wendy, lifting her in his arms and kissing her on the mouth, and she couldn't stop smiling. "I'm so glad you came, Alec." They stood with their arms around each other.

Marcus reminded himself it was none of his business what went on between Wendy and Alec, but he couldn't control the spurt of lava in his chest.

He spoke to Helen Wing, whom he knew from Sweeny's class, gesturing toward Alec. "Where'd you find him?"

Helen blushed. She was one of those girls who couldn't hide her feelings. "I heard about your story. Mr. Sweeny told us." Her eyes, her whole face shone. "I think it's wonderful."

"Don't tell him that," Alec said. "His head is too big already." He released Wendy. "You and Marcus want to cut out with us later? How about it, Marc?"

Marcus just stared at him. "No, I don't think so," he said, and walked away.

Why was he hanging around? What was he waiting for?

Was anything plainer than what he'd jus. seen? It *was* the end, it *was* over. How many times did he have to prove it to himself. *Whatever had been was over with now.* Friends? He couldn't handle it. Better to forget her, end it now, leave before he made a fool of himself.

But as he looked around for Wendy he started a farewell speech. *Wendy, you'll never . . .* Stopped himself. Nothing he said would change anything.

She was in front, near the hedge, talking to some people. He tapped her on the shoulder. "See you, Wendy."

She turned. "Marcus, are you leaving already? When am I going to see you again?"

What? It finally got to him, all this hypocrisy. "Come on, Wendy, knock it off. What do we have to see each other for?" She started to say something, but he wouldn't let her. "All this talk about being friends! You don't mean any of it." It felt so good, finally, telling her what he felt. He'd been tiptoeing around her long enough.

"You're putting it on me," she said. "You're starting to fight again."

"Look, I don't want to fight. I just came over to say good-bye. We set out to do something, we did it. I thought it was good. You didn't." He put up his hands. "So be it."

"It didn't have to end this way," she said. "It was good in the beginning, but you didn't care about my feelings."

"Feelings!" he exclaimed. "What do you know about feelings? You don't know anything, you don't see anything. I'm trying to tell you something." He spun around and walked away.

"Well, say it," she called after him. "What? What?"

He turned and looked her right in the eye. He could have hit her, she was so thick. "I love you, stupid!"

What he said stunned him. Where had that come from? He waited for her to laugh, wanted to laugh himself.

"Did you hear what you said?" Wendy said.

"I heard it."

"Do you want to say it again?"

"Do you want to hear it again?"

"Yes, I would. I really would."

"I love you, stupid."

They were walking around and he said, "Do you love me the way I love you?"

"What do you think?"

"I don't know what to think."

She put her arms around his neck and squeezed hard. "Yes, you dumbbell."

Later she said, "When did you know?"

"I didn't," he said, "not till I said it. When did you know?"

"Oh, a long time ago when we were on the hill in the park, and you said Karen's name."

"Why didn't you say it?"

"Why would I? When you said Karen's name I felt betrayed."

"Just the way I felt when I saw you with Alec."

They turned down a dark street of little stores, and rolled from doorway to doorway, kissing.

"How am I doing?" he said.

"Getting better and better."

They stopped near a model shop. There was yellow paper over the door. Inside they could see the miniature trains, and cars, and a doll's house with perfect tiny rooms. They pressed together in the doorway and kissed.

"Your eyes are open," he accused.

"So are yours."

"Mine were closed until just now."

They held hands and moved on. "What about Alec?" he said.

"What about him? Alec's a nice guy. He let me talk when I was down."

"Oh." He had to let that one go.

At dawn they went into a diner, bought a morning paper, and sat next to each other in a booth. When the waitress came they ordered sausage, eggs, and home-fries.

"I want the funnies," Wendy said.

"I always get the funnies first." He handed her the front section.

"Marco, I have to read *Doonesbury* first thing every morning."

"That's tough." But then he handed her the funnies. "I'll read the weather report."

When the waitress brought their food she made a mistake and reversed their orders. Wendy got the sausage and fries, and Marcus got the poached eggs. They waited for the waitress to leave, then Wendy reversed the plates.

They were both hungry. "Salt," he said, "Pepper."

Wendy nibbled a sausage from his plate. "This food is so good."

HARRY MAZER is a graduate of the Bronx High School of Science, Union College, and Syracuse University and is the author of many widely known books for young adults. These include *The Dollar Man, The Solid Gold Kid, The War on Villa Street,* and *The Last Mission,* the latter three ALA Notable Books. Mr. Mazer is married to Norma Fox Mazer, also a well-known writer of books for young people. The Mazers have four children and live in upstate New York.

"Literature is full of the exploits of the sexual athlete," writes Harry Mazer, "stories of relationships that are one-sided, self-absorbed, and finally unbelievable, and sad. Male sex talk is often power talk, false and misleading talk. 'Sex is easy,' the line goes; 'once you know how, that's all there is to it.' I wanted to write about another truth: how rarely the desire for sex is satisfied by sex alone. Along with sex there are other feelings: friendship and hostility, caring and anger, and even love."

"I love these home-fries," he said. "Pass the ketchup."

"Not so much," Wendy said. "I hate ketchup on my food."

"You disagree about everything, don't you."

"Pass the fries. I could say the same thing about you."

They ate. The sun rose over the rooftops. After a while Wendy handed him the funnies and he handed her the front-page news.